Destined
TO BE MINE

C J GOODYEAR

Paperback: 978-1-968667-64-1
eBook: 978-1-968667-65-8
Library of Congress Control Number: 2025918679

This is a work of fiction.

Ordering Information:

Prime Seven Media
518 Landmann St.
Tomah City, WI 54660

Printed in the United States of America

To anyone who feels as if they are not strong enough to withstand the storm, my darling, I promise you are.

Table of Contents

Authors Note

This novel covers a range of topics that may not be suitable for some readers. The main female character suffers from various mental health disorders and goes through a lot to get where she is now. If you find that you relate to some of the characters within this novel, please know that there is help available. A list of trigger warnings is listed below:

- Mentions of/explicit scenes of rape
- Mentions of/explicit scenes of sexual assault
- Bullying
- Mentions of self-harm
- Abuse (sexual, physical, emotional and psychological)
- Fear of the dark
- Fear of enclosed spaces
- Fear of spiders
- Consensual Nonconsensual sex
- Hospitals

- Death of a loved one
- Death of a parent(s)
- Stalking
- Kidnapping
- Manipulation
- Torture
- Abuse by a professional

Playlist

Panic Room by Au/Ra

Crazier Best Friend by Andi

what it means to be a girl by EMELINE

Love Me or Leave Me by Little Mix

Body by Jordan Suaste

Bears & Wolves by Lilith Max

Pretty Distraction by Skydxddy

Don't Hold Your Breath by Nicole Scherzinger

I Can Do It With a Broken Heart by Taylor Swift

To My Parents by Anna Clendening

Save You a Seat by Alex Warren

How Do I Say Goodbye by Dean Lewis

I Guess I'm In Love by Clinton Kane

Control by Zoe Wees

Little Girl Gone by CHINCHILLA

Lights Out by Mass of Man, GAWNE, Vin Jay

Cry by Benson Boone

Hold On by Chord Overstreet
I Gotcha by Cooper Alan
Better Half of Me by Tom Walker
Ordinary by Alex Warren

Chapter One

*C*hest heaving. Sweat dripping. Arms aching. Bones breaking. Blood running. Voice screaming. Empty prayers. The voice in my head screaming at me that I deserve this treatment. That I am the one to blame. A knife etches its way along my back, a blood-curdling scream escaping from my throat. My eyes roll back in my head as blood drips down onto the floor creating a disturbing pattern...

Phoebe jolts up to the sound of her alarm blaring from her phone. She groans as she frantically wipes the gunk away from her eyes and slowly pulls herself up off the bed. Another day, another shift. As Phoebe starts to stand she notices the scars on her hands, the soft pink marks making her stomach drop with disgust. Her book falls off the sofa and thuds gently onto the floor. She looks down at it, shrugs, and then walks to where her uniform is discarded in a heap on the chair nearby, deciding that her book is going to stay there until tonight. Phoebe pulls her work shirt over her head, jumps up and down trying to get into her trousers, then she dances around her flat trying to find everything before she races out the door.

The elevator down to the reception seemingly takes forever. She can feel her heart pounding in her chest, her head swimming. Gnawing at her nailbeds until they start to bleed, Phoebe assumes she's pissing off the person next to her, judging by the glares he's throwing her way. Phoebe throws her hair into a ponytail, leaving a few pieces framing her face.

That'll have to do for now, she thinks. The elevator comes to a stop and she walks across the lobby, waving to one of the regulars from the coffee shop who also lives there. His soft brown eyes meet Phoebe's for a second too long and heat rises to her cheeks, making the freckles dotted over her face stand out even more. A smile etches its way onto his face and he begins to make his way towards her. Phoebe bolts out the door and into the bustling streets of London.

Everyone jostles each other around, scowls etched onto their faces as they rush to their jobs that they hate. Phoebe on the other hand-, loves her job. She adores how fast-paced it can get and how she has gotten to know some of the regulars quite well too. Her beaten black Converse crunches over the early morning frost that covers the gum and cigarette-encased pavement. The walk to work is quick and easy if Phoebe cuts through Richmond Park, which she does every day in the mornings. As she enters the park, robins fly around the trees scavenging for any kind of last-minute berry before they hide away for winter. Her breath is visible and she huffs going up the steep slope towards her work. In her blind panic earlier, Phoebe forgot to bring her coat. She starts to shiver as the morning air seeps into her skin.

Reaching the top of the hill, she looks out across the park. The sun starts to peek through the clouds, causing the frost-covered grass to sparkle, as if sprinkled with pixie dust. Off in the distance, Phoebe sees the red bricks of *"The Magic Teapot"* emerging from between the trees. Dying roses are tied to the shop in an attempt to make the front look more lively but to no avail. Phoebe had tried talking to the manager about decorating the coffee shop to suit different times of the year. She'd decorate tables with a few fake orange leaves and have candles going at around 3 p.m. when it starts to get dark. Phoebe would also have a cute little skeleton hanging on the entry door with a few pumpkins dotted along the path for Halloween. But her boss wasn't having it and he's someone you don't want to keep pushing; Phoebe doesn't like people yelling at her.

As Phoebe reaches *"The Magic Teapot"*, the windows emit a soft glow but she can't feel the heat radiating off of the bricks as she places her hand on the old gold doorknob. Phoebe opens the yellow door with paint peeling away at the edges, its hinges squeaking in protest. The smell of coffee wafts out of the door, hitting Phoebe in the face, and she scrunches her nose up as the smell singes her nostrils.

A gentle 'ding' echoes across the room, bouncing off the wooden beams and glass windows. Conversations turn quiet as Phoebe walks to the break room to put her bag down, feeling her colleagues' judging eyes stalk her. No one talks to her apart from the customers. She gets it. If she saw someone covered in pink and white scars over their hands and a few on their cheeks she might be a bit wary too. She pulls the sleeves of her work top down, covering some of the scars on her wrists, as she moves tentatively around a few colleagues blocking the door. Her boss pins her with a look, and Phoebe shrinks away from the scrutiny of his gaze.

Phoebe pops on her little maroon apron and heads over to the coffee machine, starting to set it up before the first wave of caffeine-dependent customers come groaning through the door. The smell of freshly ground coffee fills the air around her even more, making her feeling queasy in her stomach. Phoebe checks her watch and takes a deep breath as the store opens. DING and then BANG as the customers couldn't be bothered to treat the beaten door with an ounce of respect, it ricochets off the white wall behind it. Runners in their spandex. Phoebe serves them quickly with a smile on her face without complaint, but inside her heart is going one hundred miles an hour. The anger at their actions makes her blood boil, and her face starts to heat up as she bites her tongue, not wanting to risk her job. If it was outside of work then she may say something. One of them sends a grim look towards Phoebe. Another runner looks at her crinkled up hands and cackles so loudly the windows seem to shake. They place their order with Phoebe's colleague on the tills, and Phoebe quickly makes their drinks, giving them each a small smile, refusing to acknowledge their comments. Realising that she wouldn't retaliate they take their drinks and leave, and she releases the breath that she didn't know she'd been holding.

Phoebe starts to make herself a hot chocolate when the bell goes again- it's the man that she avoided earlier- Dean. Warmth floods her cheeks as she shyly pushes her glasses up on her face, and turns to him with an awkward grin. He smiles gently at Phoebe and walks over to the till, quickly placing his order with meaning and purpose, his dark clothing blending into the dim area around them. His smooth hands lean on the counter as he orders his usual, a flat white with a design on it each day. Today Phoebe opts for a robin, her inspiration coming from the walk to work earlier.

"Was there a reason you didn't talk to me this morning Phoebe? That wasn't like you." Dean's voice washes over her like honey, smooth and calm. His eyes twinkle with mischief, but his face drops slightly when he looks at her hands as she intricately designs the robin on his coffee. Her face is contorted into concentration as her tongue sticks out a little.

"I was running late today Dean; I wasn't able to stop for a chat this morning. Plus I also looked disgusting so figured you wouldn't want to talk to me," she said, handing him his coffee, their fingers brushing ever so slightly. The warmth coming from his hands sends a jolt of surprise through Phoebe, considering that the shop's heating hasn't kicked in yet. A gentle smile creeps onto his face and he slowly sips at his drink, his tongue darting across his lips to lick the froth from them.

"You could be wearing your work uniform, a hoodie or a going-out dress; to me you'd still look amazing no matter what", Dean says with a wink and walks to his table before she can tell him how wrong he was. Phoebe goes back to work and only occasionally has a glance at Dean, seeing him typing away at his laptop and taking phone calls throughout the day. How he could be so stern and mean with whatever his job is, but so gentle and caring to people in person shocks her. She shakes her head, smiles and carries on with her job.

The rest of Phoebe's shift goes without a hitch aside from a minor incident. Dean had been on the phone to someone, yelling at whoever he was talking to. Her manager had gone over to Dean and said that if he didn't quieten down then he would be asked to leave. Dean had nodded politely but when the manager walked away, he had given him the finger and stared daggers into the back of his head. His eyes met Phoebes and they instantly softened. She smiles back and then goes back to making coffee, her eyes catching her reflection in the window as she looks at the park. The dark circles under her eyes are prominent and look lifeless. As Phoebe looks out the window, a flash of black hair comes into view, along with a menacing smile. But as Phoebe gasps and blinks, the person is gone. Shrugging it off as a hallucination due to lack of sleep, Phoebe gets on with her day, whilst trying to ignore the shivers going down her spine.

Phoebe wipes down tables as Dean comes up and stands close to her. She flinches and moves away from him, and she senses the hurt and confusion that flashes in his eyes.

"What are you doing tomorrow after work, Squidge?". Her heart beats wildly in her chest, her heart fluttering at the nickname he gave her when he first met her due to her squishy cheeks. Everyone knows that Dean has a thing for her but she was not nearly ready for a relationship. She has too much to worry about, her fear of her past catching up with her always overwhelming her. There's some stuff that she needs to keep buried there where it belongs. But he is insanely attractive, with his jet curly black hair, soft eyes and the crinkles by his mouth when he smiles. His calm demeanour washes over her and she hopes she won't get hurt as she says;

"Nothing planned but you know how Jessica is. She'll probably try and get me to go out tomorrow night." Phoebe states as she sweeps some crumbs up off of the floor with a dustpan and brush, nausea overcoming her as she finds half a bagel mushed into the floor.

"Well, can I borrow you for tomorrow then? I'm sure Jessica will understand. She's always telling you to get out more and to make some friends." Dean suggests, as he grabs a broom to the side, leaning against one of the walls.

"What were you thinking of doing?", she asks, starting to close down the coffee machine. Dean always stays until she has finished in the evening during the winter so he can walk her home. Phoebe won't deny that it is a nice feeling. Jessica, her best friend, does offer to pick her up but trying to drive through the middle of London in rush hour, in the winter, it's manic. Plus, it's not a long walk so she doesn't mind.

"I was thinking we go and get a few drinks and then maybe go to that book shop you've always wanted to try? The one where you can drink a few cocktails and pick out some books? Or you know, whatever you want to do..." It's weird to see him so shaken and nervous. He's normally so calm and collected.

"I think that's lovely; I'll tell Jessica tonight on our girls' night this evening," she says, thinking about spending time with him and also around books, her second favourite thing. He matches her excitement and leaves her be, allowing her to finish shutting up the shop.

It's around 8 pm by the time she clocks out, Dean stands close enough to her that they brush shoulders and they walk back to the flat complex, laughing and joking along the way. He walks her up to her flat and gives her an awkward side hug.

"See you tomorrow, Squidge. Wear whatever you like, you don't have to worry about impressing me. Wear whatever you feel comfortable in." He smiles at her and then walks away, his hands in his pockets for a minute. Phoebe watches, tilting her head slightly as she admires how confidently he walks. His phone rings, letting out a shrill sound and he takes it out talking to whoever is on the other end. Phoebe turns her head and starts to lock the door when she hears his voice echo from down the hall.

"I don't give a crap how you get it done, Jack, but it better be done by the time I get back to the office!", Dean's voice thunders and snaps like a whip. Phoebe's hand begins to shake and the hallway begins to spin, her breath coming out in short gasps as she pushes the door open. She closes the door and slides down onto the marble floor, the coldness soothing her burning skin. Sweat starts to drip down her forehead, her hair to stick to her face. Her heart hammers in her chest and her chest starts to ache. Feet patter across the floor and Phoebe feels someone kneel next to her as she squeezes her eyes shut and wraps her arms around herself. She rocks back and forth trying to calm herself down. Visions of her past flash behind her eyelids, and she covers her ears instead, trying to block out the sound of her screams in her head.

Jessica whispers next to her "It's fine. I heard him shouting. He's not Joel. He won't ever hurt you; Dean adores you. You're safe". Fear and exhaustion cloud Phoebe's mind and she passes out on the floor by her door.

Phoebe's eyes open and she sees herself talking to Joel. It was the night that he first ever laid hands on her. They are dancing around the kitchen, laughing at each other's goofiness and falling over the chairs seated around the table. Joel went to touch her hip but she moved away, avoiding his grasp. She giggled in response and ran to the other side of the table.

"What the fuck Phoebe? Let me touch you for Christ's sake." He sneered at her, a low growl rumbling from the back of his throat.

"I'm not in the mood Joel; I just want to goof around and then go to bed." She said politely as she moved towards him and hugged him. She wrapped his arms around him, feeling his warmth but his chest was heaving as he tried to calm down. Hot pants of air brushed the top of her head and anxiety coursed through her veins. An excruciating pain flooded her scalp as he grabbed her hair and threw her to the ground. Shock flooded her but that was replaced by even more pain as Joel's fists hit every part of her body.

"Please, Joel... stop this." She croaked out but ended up receiving a slap to the face in response. She counted the hits so she could try and focus on something. Anything to distract her from the position she is in. One... two... three... Phoebe watches herself pass out, with Joel stood over her, a murderous look in his eyes. The kind-hearted boy she used to know was long gone, replaced by a demon that would end up sucking almost all of the life out of her.

Chapter Two

After coming to, Phoebe and Jessica lie on the floor of the living room, discussing Phoebe's situation with Dean, but a knock on the door interrupts them. Phoebe looks at Jessica quizzically but then a waft of melted cheese and meat comes flowing through the underneath of the door, both of their stomachs grumbling in anticipation.

"I'll get it! I'll get it!", Jessica says as she races to the door, her pink fluffy slippers quickly plodding along the marble floor. A grin creeps its way onto her face as she hurries to pay the delivery man. His greasy black hair is sticking out from underneath his cap, his green eyes glancing around Jessica, falling to where Phoebe sat on the floor.

"'Scuse me? Here's the money for the pizza", Jessica points out, waving some money in the air around his face. His fingers come up to grab the money, but his gaze never leaves Phoebe as she twirls a strand of her between her fingers. Her white and pink scars are on display as she has changed into her pyjamas. Shorts and a tank top. The only time Phoebe feels comfortable enough wearing those clothes is when she is in her own four walls of her home.

"Oi, creep. Stop staring at her and get lost. I'm sure there are plenty of other girls who would be interested in a greaseball like you." Jessica slams the door, missing his face by a few millimetres just as Phoebe lifts her head to see what the commotion is all about. Jessica waddles back over and plops the food down on the sofa, before beginning to dig in.

"Who was at the door?" Phoebe questions as she grabs a slice, a bit of cheese dangling from her chin as she munches happily.

"Just the delivery guy. Though it was a different one than usual. Don't worry though, I sent him swiftly on his way." She digs in to eat her pizza, whilst turning the television on and scrolling through Netflix, searching for some cheesy chick flick that they can roast whilst drinking.

"I always know that I can count on you Jessica, no matter what," Phoebe says, before snatching the remote and putting on The Kissing Booth, laughing as Jessica scrunches up her nose.

"You know I am obsessed with this film, Jessica. There's nothing I can do about it; it's kind of funny looking at all the tropes of film and how cliche is". Phoebe says as she shuffles onto the sofa, draping a blanket over her leg. Jessica glances at the scars around Phoebe's ankles and nausea floods her mouth.

"Enough about the film, what is going on with your date with Dean? Why are you so nervous?" she says, deciding to ignore the feeling in her mouth and focus on Phoebe's issues.

"What if I have a panic attack and a flashback and he realises that I'm no good for him and I'm too broken for him to fix? What if he doesn't want 'used goods' per se?" Phoebe says anxiously, twirling the remote in her spare hand.

"Phoebe I love you, but that is the silliest thing I've ever heard you say. Can't you see how infatuated Dean is with you? I swear that man would burn the world for you. He would want to help you in any way that he can. He'd want you to go to therapy, to talk to him about your problems. He would want you to confront your trauma, he would do that with all the best intentions that he has. Dean would never hurt you and he would never want to make you upset". Her eyes twinkle with happiness and her shoulders relax at the thought of Phoebe being in a stable relationship in the future.

"I know that Jessica but that wouldn't stop the panic attacks from happening, the flashbacks from occurring? What would I do if I had one of those in front of Dean? I would feel so embarrassed with myself". Phoebe scrunches up her nose, her mouth twitching downwards in a frown, eyes becoming heavy with unshed tears.

"I understand that Phoebe, but you're never going to be able to get past the things that happened to you, the horrible things that you've been through unless you make the effort to try and move on with your life. That trauma is going to always be with you, yes I agree, but it's how you manage it. That will be what saves you. You don't need Dean to save you at all; you are strong enough to be able to save yourself from this and have the ability to forgive yourself for not seeing the signs sooner." Jessica smiles at her and grabs Phoebe's hand, holding it gently. Phoebe looks past Jessica, in the direction of the door.

"I swear I recognized that voice, Jessica. But maybe my paranoia is just getting the best of me," she says with a hint of distrust lacing her voice.

"I've seen pictures of Joel, if it was him then I would know. Don't worry about it, it was just another creepy guy looking for a lay." Jessica finishes munching on her slice of pizza before putting the crust down, and wiping her hands on a napkin from the pile on the side table.

Phoebe gets up and starts heading towards her bedroom, with Jessica following quickly behind. The mustard-orange four-poster bed takes up a lot of room, leaving little space for Phoebe and Jessica to move around.

"If I am going to go on this date, then I need to find something to wear that isn't leggings and a hoodie," Phoebe says with a laugh. Jessica notes the element of upset in her tone, making a mental note to take Phoebe shopping soon. She always thought that Phoebe was happy wearing either her work uniform or comfy clothes, but clearly, she was wrong. Jessica turns her attention back to Phoebe who is shuffling around in her wardrobe, huffing in frustration.

"I've got nothing to wear, everything that I own isn't good enough for a date with Dean". Phoebe pulls out a red and white spotted dress that falls to her knees, standing in front of the mirror on the wall, she turns to look at Jessica.

"That's a nice summer dress but you can't wear that in the winter Phoebe", she says with a giggle and a shake of her head.

"What do you propose I wear then clever clogs? You're the one in the fashion industry, so please, please, please, help me". Phoebe's desperate eyes meet Jessica's which sparkle with amusement.

"Let me have a look and see what we are working with in here." She walks over to the wardrobe, gently pushing Phoebe to the side. Phoebe sits on the chair placed in the front of the wardrobe, watching Jessica rummage around and chucking things out with an 'oh dear' or 'good gravy'. Phoebe's heart tightened, losing hope that there was anything worth wearing. She hadn't been on a date in years, she had been with Joel for five years but after the first year, he had stopped trying.

"Aha, here we go!", Jessica shouted, breaking Phoebe out of her daydream. Jessica pulls out some black skinny jeans, a green shirt that has buttons down the front and a black cropped leather jacket.

"I don't know Jessica; I haven't worn something like that in a long time. I don't know how confident I'd feel wearing that". Jessica rolls her eyes at the statement, and pretends she didn't hear Phoebe's complaining.

"Enough woman, now go put it on. I'll close my eyes so you don't have to worry about me seeing your back". Jessica turns away as Phoebe gets up with a huff and walks to wear the collection of clothes that have been hung over the front of the wardrobe. She begins to take her clothes off, taking a glance at Jessica, who has closed her eyes like she said. She hurriedly puts on her clothes, making sure not to glance at the scars and words embedded on her back.

"All right, I am done. You can open your eyes and see that I told you so, I look completely horrendous". Jessica turned to look at Phoebe and squealed in delight.

"Phoebe! You look fabulous! Dean is going to have a fit when he sees you!" She all but screams.

"Well I hope he doesn't have a fit, I have no medical training really", Phoebe says with a giggle, "but seriously this outfit does nothing for me, I look awful."

"Seriously Phoebe? You look incredible. The jeans fit you like a second skin, the top compliments your skin tone, and the leather jacket just makes you look like a complete badass".

"Are you sure? I don't know about this outfit; don't you think it's too revealing? What if Dean gets mad about what I am wearing?", Phoebe starts to bite on her nails and pinch her arm with the other hand.

"If you don't completely trust him or yourself, trust me. He isn't going to react that way, I bet he will be speechless, plus he has no room to give you any negative comments." Jessica says, giving Phoebe a side hug. They both look at Phoebe in the mirror but Jessica looks happy with a smile on her face, however, Phoebe is biting her lip. Her brows furrow and indecision clouds her brain.

"Hmm okay, if you say so."

"I do say so," Jessica says, then glances down at the wrist placed on her watch, "Crap! I got to go; it's getting late and I have a big presentation tomorrow. I hope you have a good shift and I'll see you around six to help you with your makeup".

"Okay Jess, I'll walk you to the door. Just make sure to text me when you get home please?"

"Of course". They walk to the door and Jessica gives Phoebe a kiss on the cheek before turning away and walking down the corridor.

After Jessica leaves, Phoebe walks back to her bedroom, after locking all the doors and making sure that all the security cameras are working, with new batteries put in just to be on the safe side. Her bed is along the back wall, far away from the window and door with two bedside tables placed on either side of the bed. On one of the tables is an iPad that Phoebe can access all the cameras in the apartment. She also can access the cameras along the hallway outside of the apartment so that she can check who's knocking at the door. Phoebe sits in bed, pulling the covers up to her shoulders, and then grabs the iPad from the table. She can't get over the feeling that it was Joel at the door earlier and he somehow knows where she is, despite her leaving the county and getting a restraining order against him. She loads up the screen, swiping back a few hours and finding the interaction between the 'pizza guy' and Jessica. However, she couldn't tell as he kept his work cap covering his eyes, successfully evading the cameras. Despite not getting a good look, Phoebe truly believes that it is him. She plays the tape thousands of times, trying to spot anything that could indicate that it was him. A ping goes off on her phone, and Phoebe quickly checks it, seeing that Jessica has just gotten home. With a heavy sigh and sleepy eyes, she puts the iPad down and closes her eyes. The unrest doesn't leave her body as she drifts off to sleep.

Joel moves around the kitchen, his eyes never meeting hers as he focuses on whatever he is doing. Phoebe looks at her laptop intently, focusing on the list of job opportunities that she has received. He hasn't spoken to her all day, not after what happened last night. Her fingers run across her cheek and her face twinges at the pain, the lump feeling tender and water floods her vision.

"I'm going out, do we need anything from the shop for the house?", his venomous voice rattles in the kitchen. She hasn't even received an apology.

"No."

"All right. No need to be such a bitch about it." Before she could think of a rebuttal, the door opened and slammed shut, the force causing the pictures to shake on the wall. A few hours seemingly passed with Phoebe clicking away on her laptop, when in reality it was only half an hour. The door gets pushed open ever so slightly, and his footsteps are quiet as he enters the house. Phoebe has her face leant on the tabletop; her glasses disregarded on one side. Her hair falls over her face as she breathes slowly, almost looking peaceful. Her face isn't scrunched up and the lines on her forehead are non-existent.

"Phoebe wake up, I've got something for you to show how sorry I am", Joel says softly as he places a hand on her shoulder, gently nudging her awake. The lines on her face come back as she stirs, her hands starting to tremble when she sees how close he is to her, his face inches away from hers.

"I wanted to show you how sorry I am, so I got you these…" From behind his back, Joel pulls out a massive bouquet, a teddy that says I love you and a box of chocolates.

"I truly am sorry for the events of last night so I'm going to take you out for dinner tonight and spoil you rotten like you deserve to be".

"Thank you, Joel, it does mean a lot to me that you are sorry". He walks behind her while she sits in the chair and hugs her from behind but when he does he takes a sneak look at her laptop something that they discussed so she would be able to have some privacy. However, he looked at her e-mail list and saw that she had been rejected from loads of jobs. Anger enveloped him and he saw red, his nostrils flat like a snake poised to attack. His arm which was hugging her then moves up to her neck, squeezing. Panic fills her body as her hands come up to try and remove his hand. He throws her to the ground and starts to repeatedly kick her side, watching her frail form curl in on itself. Her ribs protest in agony as Phoebe does her best to try and protect them. Joel leans down and forces her hands away from her ribs, before crushing them further into her body. Phoebe screams as she feels her ribs crack and dizziness overcomes her. As the world starts to go black, she feels Joel kneel next to her.

"I am sorry Phoebe; I don't know what came over me. I promise this won't happen again. I love you; I am so sorry. I'll make this up to you", his hands slide under her as he picks her up and takes her into the bedroom.

It's okay. He promises he won't do this again. He loves her, this won't happen again. He promised…

Chapter Three

Phoebe opens one eye grudgingly as the sunlight streams through the parted curtains, gently warming her face as she groans in disgust at the thought of going in for another shift this week. The alarm clock on her left beeps dramatically, Phoebe's hand quickly slamming down on it to shut it up.

"All right, all right, I'm up", she mutters angrily, stepping out of bed and stumbling towards her wardrobe. However, with a quick sniff of her armpits, she realises she needs a shower. Phoebe walks to the en suite and opens the door, dread filling her stomach. Her pulse starts to race, and her breathing becomes shallow as her mind starts to drift to panic. The water gushes out of the shower head. Her fingers dance in the water, trying to remind herself that she is the one in control. Phoebe strips out of her pyjamas and steps under the running water, trying not to get her face under it. A few droplets splash onto it anyway and she wipes them away aggressively, her heart racing even more. Phoebe breathes deeply and closes her eyes, willing herself to calm down.

"It's okay, he's not here, I am the one in control. Nothing can hurt me in these four walls", Phoebe mutters to herself. She lets her head fall on the side of the shower gently, squeezing her eyes closed as her memories threaten to overwhelm her.

Phoebe was in the shower, cleaning herself before Joel's big presentation to the firm. His development in cyber security has made him kind of famous in the computer nerd world. Phoebe isn't exactly sure what it is he does, but he had taught her how to install cameras everywhere, in his words 'to make sure you are safe and I know where you are at all times'. As she is having a shower, she can hear the distant sounds of Joel talking to some of his co-workers and laughing. She continued to scrub her body as she heard the door open, however, she knew it was Joel as he was the only other one with access to the bathroom upstairs, courtesy of the fingerprint recognition system he had installed. She felt the shower curtain move as Joel shuffled in behind her.

"Joel, I'm not in the mood. I need to get dried and dressed so I can watch your presentation and support you", she mutters as she feels his hands on her hips.

"Well I think that I need a good luck charm for my presentation, don't you?", he whispers in her ear.

"I'm not in the fucking mood Joel, don't make me tell you again", Phoebe says angrily, her hands starting to curl into fists. She hates being made to feel so weak and intimidated. Joel's hands fly up and turn her around, going up to grab her throat, and pushing her backwards until she is fully submerged underwater.

His hand tightens around her throat, Phoebe gasps for air but all she gets is water in her mouth and nose, burning her nasal passage and the back of her throat. His fingers leave her hip and start to drag dangerously close to her lower regions. A finger runs roughly up her slit, and then immense pressure is felt in her hips. She claws at his face and arms as she tries to push him away.

"Someone help me!" she screams as she feels him thrust into her harder, her screams and fights seemingly edging him on. She ignores the water flooding her vision and spewing into her mouth. His other hand comes up and grabs her hands, pinning them above her head as she continues to fight him off, refusing to give into his wicked ways.

"The walls are soundproof, no one can hear your screams", he grunts as he continues his assault. She continues to scream, in an effort that someone maybe, just maybe, be able to hear her. Joel stills in her and his hair tickles her face as he leans in close to her ear.

"If you ever tell anyone what happened or leave, I'll find you all over again and I won't let you leave. I won't be as gracious as I'm now by letting you finish your shower and then joining me on the presentation. Now hurry up and get dressed, I haven't got time for you to take forever to do your hair and makeup". He pulls out with a sneer, letting go of her wrists and throat as she falls to the floor, whimpering in pain and curling into a fetal position on the shower floor. Joel reaches over and turns the shower off, leaving her shivering on the floor, before grabbing her a towel and throwing it on her.

"I want you outside in 20 minutes, ready for the presentation. If you're not there on time, there will be hell to pay Phoebe. Don't you dare test my patience again". He leaves with heavy footsteps and the door slams with a bang as all Phoebe could do was lay there in pain as she watched him walk away.

Phoebe jumps in the shower, almost slipping over, stirring herself out of the memory. She then proceeds to shakily get out of the shower and get dressed before checking her phone, looking for any messages from her boss or any news on whether Joel is following her. Phoebe hired a private investigator a few weeks ago to ensure that she would always be one step ahead of him.

Phoebe walks to the kitchen to have some breakfast, nothing major, but wanting something before her long shift at work. Her phone rings loudly, causing her to jump in surprise. Looking down she sees that her boss is calling. She answers with a click, whilst also grabbing a protein bar from the cupboard.

"Hi Benny, I'm not late for work am I?", she says carefully, not wanting to say anything that could set him off, glancing at the clock and seeing that it was only 2 pm.

"No Phoebe, you're not late. That's actually what I wanted to talk to you about. We've had five customers all day, even though we have been open since 6 am and it's now 2 pm. We are going to shut the shop at 3 pm so there is no point in you coming in for two hours." Phoebe tries not to take this to heart as she feels her anger beginning to bubble under the surface of her skin, her hands becoming hot and sweaty as she puts her phone on speaker.

"Benny, I have rent and bills to pay. I can't afford to not have any shifts each week. I'm on a 40-hour week contract but you're barely giving me 10 hours," she begins to argue.

"I understand that Phoebe and I do feel for you. Living by yourself in London, when you're not in a relationship must be difficult for you financially. However, I can't justify having the shop open any longer."

"Okay, well I guess there's nothing that I can do to convince you to stay open, so I will see you in two days on Monday when I'm next in," she says with a sigh, the defeat encasing her body as she sits down on the sofa. She puts him on speaker as she begins to message Jessica.

"I notice you didn't mention anything in rebuttal to my comment about you being single. Why is that?" Benny said. Phoebe can hear his smirk through the phone and she bit her lip, fighting the urge to lash out at her boss, considering that she needs this job to pay for everything.

"There was nothing to say. You are correct, it is hard to be a single woman living in London, but so is living in a patriarchal society where all the men are given the shifts but the women aren't." Phoebe states with a roll of her eyes. Click. Benny hangs up on her without another word. As Phoebe's body relaxes from the call and the shower, she clicks around on her phone, applying for a few babysitting jobs for some extra money. She gets an alert on her phone from the security camera outside, pulls up the footage, looks down at the phone and drops it with a gasp. Her hands shake in anxiety, as staring directly at the camera, clear as day, is Joel. There is no mistaking his piercing eyes as they are staring through Phoebe's soul, his greasy black hair and the ominous look. Her nervous breaths fill the apartment as he waves a knife at the camera, clearly knowing that she is looking right at him as well. Her hand goes to the security button that alerts the police, but before she can press it, he shakes his head, bends down, and slides a note under her door.

Phoebe stealthily walks to the door, constantly keeping her eye on the camera footage as she picks up the note. She unfolds it quickly, with the other hand making sure all the doors are locked. She reads the note with a shaky breath;

'Don't think about reporting me to the police. I don't care about you having a restraining order on me. I'll always be around, waiting and watching.'

She glances back at the phone, noting that she had managed to leave a few scars on his face from the last time she escaped him. Self-pride blooms in Phoebe's chest at the thought of her fighting back so hard and never giving up. With a wicked scheming smile, he tilts his head and leaves. The tightness in her chest lessens, her heart rate slows down, and the pounding in her ear dulls to a light throb. She clicks on her call button and phones the first person she thinks of.

"Hello Phoebe? Is everything okay? You never ring me", his gentle tone calming her as she listens to his voice, almost forgetting that he has asked her a question.

"Dean. I'm okay, I just needed to hear your voice", her voice quivering and a few tears start to trickle down her face; the whole interaction slowly catching up to her.

"Talk to me Squidge, what's wrong? I can tell you are crying", his voice becomes a bit firm.

"I'll be okay, I'm just a bit shaken up. Someone from my past has found me, I don't know where to go. Nowhere is safe." Phoebe's voice shakes as she speaks, pacing the living room floor and the room tilting as a wave of dizziness crashes into her.

"I'll be at yours in 20. Have a bag packed, I'll take you somewhere off the grid, no questions asked. We can still go for our date night, but I'll have security guarding the exits. Who are you running from so I know who we are dealing with?" A sense of safety and security overcomes Phoebe, calmness running through her veins, simmering the uncontrolled rage and panic within her body. The thought of Joel finding her scares her but enrages her more. She had covered her tracks, changed her name, and got new accounts for everything. How had Joel found her? Did he have help? There was Pitch but he wasn't the brightest spark in the tool box, it had to be someone else.

"Joel Rogue."

"Well, he even sounds like a dickhead," Dean says with a laugh, trying to lighten the mood.

"Yeh, I guess, I wish I had figured that out long before I dated him," Phoebe half-heartedly laughs back.

"Ahhh, the jealous ex cliché. I can't wait to see how this unfolds," a playful edge to his voice.

"No, it's not like that at all. Why do men always think that way?", Phoebe says with a dismissive tone, bristling slightly at his words.

"I'm sorry Phoebe, I didn't mean to assume. I promise you can tell me anything and as much as you feel comfortable with tonight. There is absolutely no pressure." Dean's voice fills with sincerity and Phoebe stumbles as his words catch her off guard.

"I'll see you soon, I am going to go pack", she says bluntly before abruptly ending the call, slamming her phone down onto a side table.

God, that was rude of me, she thinks before sprinting to her room, grabbing a bag and shovelling a bunch of clothes in there, along with her hairbrush, hair ties and a few other accessories. Phoebe eyes the outfit hung over her chair in the corner, before grabbing it and placing it at the top of her bag, zipping it shut before walking back out into the living room and grabbing her iPad, and putting it in her bag as well.

As Phoebe paces around the apartment, she ponders the thought about how Joel found her. She had done everything the police had told her to do to keep her true identity safe, but someone in the department must've been close to him. Before everything went south in their relationship, Phoebe ignored the red flags and only saw the good in him, thinking that he was the best thing in the world. But, all of that was lying and deceitful. Joel had the whole town on his side, he blamed everything that went wrong in the relationship on Phoebe, claiming that she never gave him what he needed. She had left her family for him, and all her friends. Phoebe pretended to be someone that she was not, and yet that was still not good enough for him.

Phoebe pulls herself out of her daydream when the doorbell goes and checks the camera before answering the door. It's Dean. He wraps his arms around her, squeezing her not too tightly, but tight enough for her to feel safe. Phoebe relaxes into his arms and lets the tears fall onto his black shirt.

"It's okay, you're safe. No one can hurt you whilst I'm with you, I promise Squidge." The stress of the day overwhelms her body and she collapses in his arms, darkness beckoning her.

Dean carries her to his car, her bag swung over his shoulder, and gently places her in the passenger seat before plugging her in. He walks round to the driver's side, determination on his face as he starts the car and drives them to his other apartment. Dean carries Phoebe upstairs, ignoring the questioning looks from people in the parking lot and reception of the building. The elevator dings open and Dean waits as staff members rush out as the day has come to an end, all of them jostling each other as they race to get home to see their families. Dean's heart clenches at the thought of a family, but he shoves it to the side as Phoebe stirs in her sleep, her eyebrows furrowing and a small whimper falls from her parted lips. Dean's eyes darken as he wonders what this Joel character has done to hurt Phoebe this much and scare her to the point she passed out in his arms. The elevator doors open into Dean's apartment, the warm lights flooding the space, as Dean walks through the living room, gently nudging his bedroom door open with his boot, before placing Phoebe on the bed, pulling the covers up and resting just under her chin. He smiles warmly before grabbing a pillow from the top of the bed and walking over to a chair in the corner, sitting down and placing the pillow behind his head. As he watches over Phoebe, his eyes begin to droop and he falls asleep in the chair.

Chapter Four

Phoebe feels a dip below her as the mattress shifts with a new added weight. A hand caresses her face gently, causing Phoebe to nuzzle into it briefly. Then with a jump and a gasp, remembering the events of yesterday, she rolls ungracefully out of the bed, her feet hitting the soft carpet and she almost groans in happiness.

"Squidge, it's just me. You're safe, it's not Joel," a quiet voice says from the bed. Phoebe looks over to the bed seeing Dean sitting on the bed, leaning back slightly, a small smile curling its way on his face. His arms strain against the tightness of his grey shirt, blending in beautifully with his low-waist joggers. His hair remains untamed and dishevelled, his eyes still droopy from only just waking up before Phoebe.

"Where are we?," she asks curiously, feeling uneasy with not knowing where they are.

"My other apartment, which is at a high security multiplex. Only myself, my two main bodyguards and now you know about this other apartment." Dean says with a small smile, his eyes twinkling. Phoebe blushes as he stares at her intensely, whilst she looks around at the apartment, through the door of the bedroom; a small living room off to one side and a kitchen and a bathroom off to the other side. The whole apartment is designed with rustic wooden furniture, with red and black details everywhere.

"Nowhere is safe. He will always find me," Phoebe says shakily as she begins to pace up and down the bedroom, running her fingers through her hair, pulling it slightly, before she takes in the chair tucked into the corner of the room, a pillow and blanket laying haphazardly on the arm of the chair. Phoebe turns to look at Dean, a questioning look on her face.

"Who's going to find you? I'm guessing you're talking about Joel?" Also, yes I slept in the chair for a few hours whilst you were passed out, I didn't want to disturb you", a stern look covers Dean's face as he waits for Phoebe to answer. He stays sat on the bed but leans forward so his arms are resting on his legs. Dean stares intently at Phoebe as she wrings her hands, debating whether to tell him or not. Her forehead drips with sweat and her heart thumps at the thought of Dean sleeping in the chair.

"Yes. So... about a year ago... I finally decided to leave that relationship as it wasn't working..."

"And?"

"And Joel hurt me in more ways than anyone ever has in my life. I don't want to tell you all the details just yet. But he is looking for me, and I know that if he ever gets his hands on me then you'll never see me again." Tears stream down Phoebe's face, Dean gets up slowly, walks over to her and gently brushes the hair away from her face with one hand, whilst the other gently removes the tears falling from her eyes.

"Phoebe, I won't ever probe you for details. Ever. But please know that you can trust me. I know it'll take time and effort on my part but I just want you to know that." As Phoebe looks into his eyes, she can see the sincerity in them, the gentle eyes gazing back at her.

"I trust you Dean, but not completely. I still would very much like to go on that date with you," she says as she grabs his hand, knowing that he probably won't ever hurt her. Jessica was right, she needs to take a leap of faith and believe that not everyone is like Joel.

"Of course, we can still go on our date. I've booked us reservations at Books & Booze for 7 pm. That gives you an hour to get ready, I know that you like to have plans told to you so I took the liberty of organizing this for us. Is that okay?" Dean asks, almost unsure that he has done the right thing by taking charge.

"Yes, I can work with that, I like you taking charge Dean, I find it kind of sexy," Phoebe says with a giggle as she looks up through her lashes at him. He laughs smoothly, then nudges her towards the bathroom.

"Go get dressed and ready for tonight. I know you'll look amazing Phoebe," Dean says with a soft tone as he walks out of the bedroom and into the kitchen. Phoebe blushes slightly, picks up her clothes that she and Jessica decided on the night before, and walks to the bathroom. She quickly gets changed, however, decides not to put on her leather jacket as she knows that she and Dean will be inside for most of the night. Within the hour, Phoebe manages to get ready and together they take the elevator downstairs and joins Dean in his car, him keeping a hand on hers the whole ride to the bar.

The red bricks of *Books & Booze* stand out in contrast to the pale white buildings surrounding it. Fairy lights twinkle in the windows as Phoebe stares up at the building in awe. The door opens with a gentle jingle, the warmth from the shop enveloping Phoebe and Dean as they walk in, slightly fogging up her glasses. She pulls them off her face and rests them on the top of her head. The walls are covered in bookcases, from the floor to the ceiling with rolling ladders attached to them. Phoebe walks over to one section of the books and runs her fingers along the soft leather, smiling as she turns to look back at Dean, but he's already staring at her. Their eyes meet and Phoebe blushes but only for a second as she takes in the crystal chandeliers along the ceiling, softly illuminating the bar where Dean stands. Phoebe walks over to him and slots her hand into his, a warmth spreading through her chest, feeling as though her hand is made for his as they fit perfectly together. His fingers twitch interlaced with hers but he doesn't try to pull away.

"What drink would you like, Phoebe? Whatever you want and you can have it," Dean says as the bartender waits somewhat impatiently as Phoebe browses the menu.

"I think I'll just have a Sex on the Beach for now Dean, but I might try a new one later if that's okay?" The bartender nods at her before turning to Dean.

"I'll have what she's having, but can you make it alcohol free since I'm driving please?" He asks the bartender politely. After ordering their drinks, they are directed to a small table in the back corner, hidden away from everyone, but still with eyes on the door. Phoebe notes two men loitering at the two exit doors, one with dirty blonde hair and one with jet black hair, both muscly and scanning the crowd every once in a while, before their eyes settle back on Phoebe and Dean. Dean catches her gaze and looks over to the corners.

"Ah that's just Leon and Jack, my two best security guards and best friends. They are just here to make sure we are safe and also to grill me about the date later on." Phoebe giggles and nods at them, giving them a small wave and the corners of their lips quirk up as they nod back.

As the night continues with Phoebe sipping on cocktails and Dean drinking mocktails, unbeknown to each other, they keep making sideway glances at one another as they read the first chapter of a number of books. Phoebe's piles of books are significantly higher than Dean's, focusing mainly on dragons and fairies. However, Dean's is distinguishably different as he seems fond of murder and horror novels.

"Hello, can we please have the bill when you get five minutes?" Dean asks a kind smile towards the waiter, ignoring the little glare that Phoebe swiftly sends his way.

"Absolutely sir, I will grab that for you now." The waiter hastily walks away, almost knocking into one of the chairs.

"You know, I can pay for my own drinks and books?," Phoebe says as she looks at the small pile of fantasy romance books placed on the side next to her drinks.

"I know, I know. But I was bought up to believe that the gentleman always pays for the first date. Anyways, if it means that much to you, you can buy everything for the next date."

"Oh? There's going to be a second date is there?" Phoebe raises an eyebrow, watching as Dean's face pales.

"Well... I... uh... at least hope there's one more..." he stutters and stammers, straightening his shirt and rubbing his hand on the back of his neck.

"You know what? Come to think of it, I'd like that a lot too Dean. I don't really want the night to end just yet. How about we walk up to St Paul's Cathedral, it's not too far from here?" He nods in agreement, proceeds to pay the bill, takes her hand and together they walk out into the night.

As Phoebe and Dean stand hand in hand whilst looking at the soft yellow lights lighting up St Paul's Cathedral, Dean's phone lets out an almighty ring. With a soft sigh, Phoebe pulls her hand out of Dean's and wraps her arms around herself, moving away quickly to give him space. She knew better than to interrupt men when they were busy with work.

"Sorry Squidge, I have to take this. I hope that's okay. If you see anyone that looks like Joel, just give Jack or Leon a shout, and they will come running", he says as he already starts to take his phone out of his pocket.

"It's okay, I don't mind, I'll be standing by the bridge," Phoebe says softly as she walks away, Dean smiling gently.

"Hello? Yes, speaking. Do you know where they are?" Dean grunts out sternly, his brows furrowing as he listens to whoever is on the other end of the phone.

"What do you mean you can't find him, apparently he has no reason to hide if he showed his face on a camera"... Dean's nostrils flare in anger, his voice cracking rage "I don't care how long it takes, fucking find him!" Dean screams the last word as his hand goes up to his hair, yanking in frustration. He turns to go back round to Phoebe and his face drops when he sees that she is on the ground on her knees, tears streaming down her face as she looks at him in anguish and despair.

"Squidge? You okay? What's wrong? You look like you've seen a ghost." Dean says apprehensively, taking slow steps towards her as onlookers ignore them as they walk past. Phoebe doesn't respond, just continues to look at him in horror and almost with disgust. Her eyes widen and she looks past him, staring off at something in the distance.

"I don't know what's going on but you're safe Phoebe, you're okay," he says from a distance, crouching down to her level but keeping a respectable space away.

"Don't fucking lie to me, Phoebe! I know you lied to me; I know you went out last night. Who the fuck were you with? I bet you were cheating on me like the slut you are!" Joel's hand came

soaring down on her face, the slap echoing throughout the empty halls of their old house.

Phoebe whimpers as the flashbacks invade her senses, her cheek stinging with old pain resurfacing. Dean watches on, too scared to do anything, not sure how he can help with whatever Phoebe is going through.

"I didn't do anything, I swear Joel. I just went out with Jessica to the bar, then I headed straight back here. There's nothing else that happened," Phoebe screams as Joel repeatedly slaps her face, before throwing her to the ground, Phoebe gasping in pain as her ribs slam against the floor.

Dean watches her hands begin to shake, her breathing becoming laboured as panic starts to set into her senses and body.

Joel reaches over, grabbing a knife from the table before hoisting Phoebe up onto it, laying her down flat on her stomach, taking care to avoid her flailing limbs. One hand starts to lift her top, the other holding down her neck, finding the control empowering as Joel moves the knife slowly down her back.

Whimpers start to flood the bridge as Phoebe screws her eyes shut as she tries to escape the horrors of her past. Dean motions to Jack and Leon to come over with his fingers, being careful not to raise his voice.

"I don't know what Joel did, but you are safe here. I would never hurt you, I'm sorry I raised my voice. Please tell me what I can do to help you." Phoebe can hear his voice in her head as she tries to focus on it rather than the vivid memories playing in her brain. He goes to touch her arm, but she flinches so hard that

Dean draws his hand away quickly, almost as if he is touching hot lava.

Phoebe screams as she feels the knife dig into her back, slowly gliding down the silky smooth feel of her skin. Joel laughs above her as he continues his relentless pace, moving the knife in this way and that. Phoebe tries to twist her head around to look at her back, to try and see what he is carving there. But Joel slams her head to the side of the table.

"You'll see when I'm done, and then no one will ever question who you belong to," Joel answered as he continued his assault. He kept up with his torturous pace as Phoebe lay there sobbing in agony. After what feels like an eternity, Joel pulls Phoebe from the table, keeping one arm around her waist to keep her upright as he drags her to the mirror.

"Phoebe you are safe. He is not here." Phoebe can hear Dean speaking but she can't pull herself away from the flashback, as much as she did not want to relive it.

"Stand there and don't move," he says sternly as he walks away to grab something else. Phoebe's legs threaten to give way, but she refuses to give Joel any more ammunition. He returns with another mirror and holds it up to her back so she can see her back in the mirror in front of her. There, scribbled in giant capital letters into the flesh of her back, is the name Joel.

"Please come back to me Phoebe, I want to help you through this". Dean's soft voice continues to flood her memory, and the flashback begins to fade as she opens her eyes, finding Dean watching her like a hawk. He is knelt down on the ground like she is, but staying a few metres back. Phoebe begins to shiver with cold and dread, her teeth chattering with the wind and anxiety.

"Phoebe, is it okay if I come close to you?" Dean asks. She nods in agreement, him moving closer to her and draping his jacket around her shoulders.

"What if you get cold?" Phoebe asks with a timid look on her face, not wanting Dean to get sick.

"I'll be fine Squidge, let's just focus on getting you home in the warm okay?" he suggests. Phoebe nuzzles into the warmth and Dean begins to lead her to the car that he got his bodyguards to bring around for him. He pops her into the passenger side and walks to his side, but not before having one last look around. Dean sees something in the shadows but thinks nothing of it and drives off, knowing they will be safe at his apartment. The heat from the radiator floods the car, Phoebe's breath evening out but her eyes stay glassy as she reaches for Deans hand. His fingers twitch as he adjust his grip on the steering wheel, knuckles turning white. Her face pales at the rejection but she says nothing, staring out the windows, watching the lights as they zoom by. He silently drives them back to the apartment and sets the car in park. He slowly gets out of the car and as Phoebe does to get out, he opens the door and offers her his hand. They walk up to the reception and ride the elevator, the silence between them almost deafening.

Chapter Five

Once they enter the apartment, Dean walks towards the kitchen and sets the kettle to boil. Phoebe stands on the edge of the kitchen, fiddling with her fingers and her eyes darting around anxiously. They settle back on Dean and watches as he methodically makes himself a cup of coffee and heats up some milk for Phoebe's hot chocolate. Phoebe notices that he knows exactly what she orders, but doesn't say anything, content in just watching him for now. Dean's hands move without thinking as he stirs his black coffee, before staring at it and then adding another heap of coffee to it.

"I thought that you'd be one of those people that has a fancy coffee machine in their kitchen," Phoebe says nervously, biting at her bottom lip as she watches him warily. Dean offers her a small smile as he adds squirty cream to Phoebe's cup, a blush slowly painting his cheeks a soft pink.

"I used to, but I hardly used it so I gave it away to someone who needed it more and could use it. All the buttons and everything confused me." He explains bashfully.

"That's a shame, I could have taught you how to make an amazing cappuccino or a flat white," she suggests as she takes a step towards him apprehensively. His eyes flick to hers, the darkness in them making her breath catch in her chest. He nods towards two dark green sofas in the corner facing each other, with a little oak coffee table in-between them. They both move over and sit down before taking a sip of their drinks, happily sighing at the warmth flooding their bodies. Dean watches her from the corner of his eye before setting his drink down on the coaster.

"I'm not asking for a lot from you Squidge, but is there anything you can tell me about your past that can help me understand and support you? Only tell me what you feel comfortable with, but I want to help you." Phoebe holds the cup between her hands as she takes a sip, calming her down as her eyes flash with uncertainty at Dean's proposal.

"What if I tell you something about my past and then you tell me something about you.? I don't really know that much about you and I have kind of trusted you blindly not to kill me or something." Her forehead furrows as she watches Dean, waiting for him to decline and for her to bolt for the doors. To her surprise, he nods and settles back in the chair, his muscles flexing as he tries to relax.

"I think that's a fair compromise. Okay, my name is Dean Archer, I'm twenty-seven years old and I am a CEO of my own company." He takes another sip of his coffee, some life returning back to his face.

"Okay, I have a very troubled past, but to start off, my favourite colour is dark green, I'm twenty-three and my favourite animal is a starfish," Phoebe says whilst Dean nods before ushering her to continue, "I met my ex-fiancé when I was seventeen years old and he was twenty-two, so he would be twenty-eight now. At first everything was amazing between us, my parents didn't approve and we would constantly fight about. But they let me date him because they knew I was hurting and needed someone in my life." She lets out a shaky breath, takes a sip of her hot chocolate but doesn't look over at him. She doesn't need his pity, as she begins to open up a little, shifting in her seat.

"I wanted to move in with him, but my parents said no. It was the one and only time they really put their foot down with me, but at the time I hated them. I called up... this person... and explained everything to them, and then they picked me up from the end of the street and we went back to his. That was the first time he ever laid a hand on me, all because my parents wouldn't let me live with him. But it didn't matter what they said, because the following day I was contacted by the police. It turns out that night, they had been burgled and it had gone wrong and the robber had shot them. The last thing I said to them was that I hated them. I didn't think about it at the time, but now, I have a feeling that Joel was involved with getting rid of them... but I could never prove it." Phoebe lets out a deep breath and takes a risk looking at Dean, his head resting on his chin. Phoebe's blood boils as she thinks he is asleep but his head rises and tears are streaming down his face.

"I'm so sorry Phoebe, no one should have to deal with that. I can't even begin to imagine how you must have felt or continue to feel," his hand twitches to reach for her but stays on the arm of the chair. Phoebe brushes a stray hair out of her face and pushes her glasses higher up her face. Dean notices there are no tears in her eyes and makes a mental note to ask about that at a later date.

"Do you know where you're parents are buried?" Dean asks warily.

"Yes, I used to try and go to visit them once every two weeks but I haven't been for almost a year since I escaped Joel's clutches. I couldn't risk him finding out where they are buried as I wasn't sure how he would react."

"Was your relationship with you parents good before meeting Joel?", Dean asks, not sure how to deal with either answer but his heart hammers in his chest at the sight of this lovely girl going through so much and so quickly, never having time to deal with it or compartmentalise it. She smiles softly, her eyes unfocusing as she reminisces.

"It was the best, we were like best friends, as I didn't have many growing up. Sure, we would have arguments like any family, but we would always find a way back to each other. I never had to fight for their love, even when I felt like I didn't deserve it." Tears start to peak in at the corners of her eyes but she blinks them away, refusing to let them fall. "When I started dating Joel, it was like they didn't know who I was anymore, like I wasn't something that needed to be protected. I was going out nearly every night and going off to random fields to get drunk and have sex. When I would have some time free to do things with them, they would shut me down or refuse to talk to me, even though that was the time I needed them the most. I was raped in their own house, but I felt like I couldn't tell them because they would just say 'I told you not to get with him' or something along those lines. But they were both hurting after we lost my Grandad, so I tried not to hold it against them." Tears stream down both their faces and Dean rests his hand on top of Phoebe's, not holding it just yet but letting her know he is there. Phoebe's heart pounds in her chest and she pushes one hand into her eyes, trying to fight off the flashback that is coming. Sweat encases her body and she slowly rises to her feet before walking off to Dean's bedroom, hearing the soft patter of his feet as he follows her not too closely behind.

"I promise to never hurt you or leave you Squidge, I am not going to go anywhere just because you have told me all of this. It doesn't change who you are as a person", he says quietly as he watches her sit gently on the bed, her fingers running over the soft duvet and her feet rubbing the rug on the floor. She hums but Dean can tell that she doesn't believe her, her eyes glassy as she looks around his bedroom, taking in the dark furniture and dark green walls. Dean walks around the bedroom to one of his chests of drawers, watering the flowers on top of them. Lilies, tulips, orchids, dahlias and peonies all organised in colour order. A few leafy plants hang from the ceiling and Phoebe nestles into the bed as he waters them too, before placing the watering can back in its place by the door, before writing a label and sticking it on it, saying 'fill me'. Dean sits on the chair in the corner of the room and picks up a book.

"What are you doing? This is your room, if you want to get into bed then you can, you don't need to worry about me."

"Whilst it may be my bed, I wouldn't feel comfortable joining you just yet. You need sleep and I'm quite content sitting over here and reading, don't worry about me," he says with a cheesy grin as he throws her statement back at her, before wiggling his behind and getting comfier in the chair. Phoebe lets out a yawn before slamming a hand over her mouth and looking at Dean with a sheepish grin. He gives her a knowing smile before opening his book, and Phoebe notices it's one of the ones she picked up from their first date at *Books & Booze*. Her eyes drift shut as she falls into a slumber.

Chapter Six

A knife scratches down Phoebe's back as she screams in pain. Joel's eye glint dangerously in the mirror as he stares at Phoebe's pain ridden face. Joel runs his fingers over the scars covering her back and legs as she is strapped down to the table.

"I wouldn't have to do this if you had just listened to me, Phoebe. I don't like hurting you but you give me no choice when you act like a child," Joel says condescendingly. Phoebe whimpers in agony but bites on her tongue, knowing she will say something that will get her in trouble. Joel walks over to the table of instruments to the side of them, and picks up something. Phoebe tries to move her head to look, but the strap on the back of her head presses down tightly, rendering her immobile. A crack of a whip fills the air and Phoebe lets out a blood curdling scream despite her best efforts to not show weakness. Joel walks round the front of the table and crouches intimidatingly in front of her, glaring daggers into her soul. She pulls on the restraints as she feels her skin splitting and blood oozing onto the floor below her.

"You need to behave Phoebe, I can't have people knowing what goes on behind closed doors. Do you think you can behave for me, sweet girl?" His face never leaves her eyes and he squints dangerously as Phoebe rasps out.

"I will never stop fighting you, I will find a way out even if the only way is through death." She begins to pull harder on the restraints, them digging into her skin even further and Joel stands up without a word, the whip trailing gently on the blood stricken floor as he walks round the table. The whip lashes down with cool and calm precision, each crack of the whip startling Phoebe and she screams until her voice grows hoarse. Joel wraps the whip around her neck and pulls it tight as he shoves down his trousers and boxers, forcing himself into her as she gasps for breath.

"Phoebe… Phoebe… Squidge, can you hear me?…"

Phoebe wakes up with a bolt and starts throwing punches and kicks, screaming at the top of her lungs; but she ends up being pinned to the bed.

"Get off of me, leave me alone, I don't want to go back to him!" She thrashes against the grip on her shoulders and attempts to bite at the hands.

"Phoebe it's okay, you're safe now, no one can hurt you. I'm holding you down so you don't hurt yourself." A voice says gently, the pressure on her arms easing slightly.

"Dean?", she says with a whimper, embarrassment flooding her body and her face goes red.

"Yes Squidge, it's me. You were having a nightmare, and started fighting in your sleep." Dean slowly lets go of her arms and helps her into a seating position, scanning her face for any injuries, his book laying open on the floor.

"Flashback. I get them a lot."

"It's okay, we've all got our trauma. What can I do to help?" Dean says softly as he slowly moves off of her, sitting up within arm's reach if needed. Phoebe shuffles in the bed, pulling the duvet up to her chin as she watches Dean warily.

"I want to learn to protect myself. I'm tired of living my life in fear that Joel is hunting me." She eyes Dean sceptically, assuming that he will say no. He looks at her for a few minutes before nodding, slowly reaching out a hand and Phoebe grabs it without hesitation, a small smile forming on both their faces.

"Alright, we can do that. But would you feel more comfortable me training you? It won't be easy, not like the women you read about in your books where they become so powerful overnight. This is going to take a lot of time and patience and hard work. If you do this, I'd also like to suggest that you see a therapist, I can recommend the one I'm seeing, she is very good and very respected in her field." Phoebe lets out a giggle at the comment about the books she reads, before pondering the rest of what Dean said. She nods slowly but terror crosses her face at the idea of going to a therapist, and Dean reads her like an open book.

"I know it's hard making that first step, but as much as I want to help you, there are some things that I am not trained in. I can be an ear for you to rant to, but in order for you to heal, I think a therapists help would be more beneficial." Phoebe nods again and agrees. She slowly moves closer to Dean and gives him a soft peck on the cheek, before rising out of the bed and grabbing one of his tops and shorts. Dean looks at her in bewilderment and Phoebe lets out a hearty laugh at his face.

"Well there's no time like the present! Plus, I don't have any workout clothes here so yours will have to do for now," she says with a smile as she rapidly gets dressed as she feels Deans eyes run briefly over her scars but not lingering. When she turns to look at him, there's no disgust on his face and her heart warms slightly at that fact.

Dean rises from the bed as well and they walk down to the apartment gym, Dean giving everyone a stern look before most of them leave. One man stays sat on a bench, curling a weight to his chest. His black hair sticks to his head from being drenched in sweat, and the cap on his head has the sides soaked as well. His eyes stay stuck to the floor even as Dean clears his throat.

"Hey mate, you know the rules. I'm in here, so that means you're not," he says harshly and Phoebe's eyes grow big as she stares at Dean in shock at his tone. The man rises from the bench and walks to the door but his arm brushes up against Phoebe's as he knocks into her. Shivers run up her spine and goosebumps cover her arms. Dean goes to move after him but Phoebe grabs his arm and shakes her head gently.

"It's fine Dean, let's just get started on the training. The sooner I can defend myself and not have to rely on anyone else, the better." Dean bristles slightly at her words but doesn't say anything, just nods and moves them onto the sparring mats in the middle of the room. As they move, Phoebe takes a look at the gym, with its high ceiling, big windows and an impressive variety of weights and exercise machines all around the walls.

"Okay, so first things first. I want to see what you know and if you can get out of any of these positions. I'll run through them with you twice each, and then on the third time, I'd like you to be able to escape from the positions. If that doesn't work, then we will go through them again until you can do them. We won't move onto the next stage until you have perfected theses manoeuvres, is that okay?" Despite his harsh tone, Phoebe knows Dean cares about her and the bluntness of his tone shows he is taking her safety seriously. Phoebes heart flutters in her chest and she pushes the slight panic down into a locked box.

"This definitely isn't like the books I read" she laughs and the corners of Deans mouth turn up slightly. He shakes his head at her, not in annoyance and he instructs her to get into position, telling her how to angle her body and put more or less weight on each foot.

"You're small but you can use that to your advantage Squidge. Your frame allows you to dodge attacks and gives you the chance to escape. You probably won't be able to take down a fully grown man, but you can put some distance between you and your attacker. If you find yourself in close proximity, then aim for the persons lower areas, throat or forehead." Dean moves behind her and grabs her neck in a chokehold but not hard enough to hurt her, and Phoebe quickly throws an elbow back, catching Dean off guard, allowing her to twirl out of his hold. He nods as he looks at her, but notices she's favouring her left leg, so quickly swipes her right out from under her. Phoebe lands on the mat with a groan and Dean stands over her.

"Never let your guard down Squidge." He says with a small smirk. Phoebe rolls over and kicks Dean in the crotch and he lets out a huff of air as he's brought to his knees in pain. Phoebe makes sure to put some space between them, fear slowly creeping onto her face as Dean glares slightly at her. He shakes his head, and the building rage passes and his cool demeanour returns. Phoebe eyes him and takes another step back off of the mat, before grabbing a bottle of water from the side.

"Sorry Squidge, I got lost in the moment for a second there. Once you've had a drink, let's do a bit of cardio and see how much work we need to do." Phoebe nods at him and they move onto the treadmills, and they both start off at a slow pace before Dean increases both of theirs, and they run at that constant speed for about twenty minutes.

"You need to be able to keep the same pace as me but last longer if you want to have any chance of escaping someone chasing you," he says as he looks at Phoebe who is panting and sweat dripping from her head onto her eyebrows and down her cheeks, leaving a salty trail in its wake. She hastily wipes the sweat away and focuses on breathing steadily as much as she can. Her stomach turns and her hands grow cold, so she quickly stops the treadmill, leans over the railing, and throws up on the floor.

"Shit Phoebe! Are you okay?", Dean exclaims as he slams on the emergency brake on his treadmill, jumping off before it completely stops to run around to move her hair out of her face, carefully avoiding stepping in the sick. Another wave of sickness covers the floor and some drops onto Dean's shoes but he pays it no mind as his focus is on Phoebe.

"I'm so proud of you for staying on as long as you did Squidge, I seriously underestimated you as I didn't think you'd be able to manage. How about we call it here for the day and we get you cleaned up, and we can do whatever you want for the rest of the day. I have to make a phone call but I can do that whilst you have a shower."

Phoebe raises her head to look at where he is crouched in front of her, tears streaming down her face. He moves to brush them away with the pads of his thumbs, but she lets out a terrified whimper and he quickly retracts his hand. Phoebe pulls the sleeves on Dean's top down and wipes the tears away herself before pushing off of the railing and slowly moving towards the door to go back upstairs. When it doesn't open, she turns to look at Dean, raising her eyebrows as he laughs slightly.

"You don't live here Squidge, this block of flats is different to the one you live in. The doors only open if you rent or own an apartment here. Or in my case, if I own the block of flats. I only live at that one sometimes so I have an excuse to see you." Phoebe just blinks at him, completely thrown off that he would buy an apartment so that he could see her. A blush creeps up her neck and across her cheeks as she watches Dean pick up the bottles of water before grabbing his phone.

"Jack, hey buddy. Could we have a cleaning team sent down to the gym please, I pushed myself too hard on the treadmill and had a slight incident... you know me, always trying to be better... uh huh... okay, can you also get Fiona to cancel my appointments for today please? I've had something come up and that takes priority today... Thanks dude, and yeah let's get together at some point so that I can whoop your ass at darts again. Alright, talk later. Bye". Phoebe stares at him in bewilderment but then, very slowly, she places her hand in his and together they walk out of the gym and into the elevator back to Dean's apartment on the top floor. As the lift ascends, Phoebe looks out the windows and sees *The Magic Teapot* in the distance, her heart hammering at the thought of never working there again, even if she did have to work for the misogynistic manager. She sighs softly but turns away to face Dean, finding him already looking at her with a twinkle in his eye.

The elevator arrives with a ding, and they step out into Dean's living room, slowly making their way to the shower, careful not to move too quickly so Phoebe doesn't lose the contents of her stomach again. Dean places Phoebe on the tub near the bath, and as he runs his hands under the water once he's turned the shower on, Phoebe looks at the bathroom. Soft yellow tiles cover the wall, and the lights are a soft amber colour, not to harsh and make her heart warm in happiness that she doesn't have to deal with bright lighting. The shower head is powerful and she watches intently as Dean adjust the temperature to the right setting. He steps away and helps Phoebe stand in the shower but doesn't touch her clothing. He steps out of the shower and closes the curtain.

"Do you want me to leave or stay on the outside of the curtain Squidge?"

"Can you stay out there please? I don't want to be alone right now." She places her fingers in the water, testing the temperature, before then placing her legs under the powerful stream. Phoebe strips quickly and places the clothes at the edge of the bath, watching intently as they disappear from view as Dean places them in the laundry basket.

"Of course Darling." Beyond the curtain, Dean sits on a small box to the side of the bathroom, and scrolls on his phone, seeing if any of his team have located Joel.

She lathers herself in soap, the musky scent that is just Dean floods her nostrils and threatens to overwhelm her senses. She takes a few breaths to steady herself before washing the sick out of her hair and then moving onto shave her legs. For the first time in four years, Phoebe manages to have a shower without a flashback, and she breathes a sigh of relief at Dean not having to deal with that. Once she's finished, the shower turns off and the curtain is pulled back but all that Phoebe sees is a fluffy white towel and Dean facing the door. She takes the towel off of him and quickly wraps it around herself before stepping out of the tub and tapping Dean on the shoulder. He turns just in time to see red hair lurch towards his chest as he feels Phoebes arms tightly wrap around him. He hums in happiness and breaths the apple scent from her hair before nuzzling into it, ignoring the fact that it is dripping water all over the floor. For the first time in his life, Dean feels comfortable not doing anything and just holding Phoebe in his arms, the first time she has willingly hugged him. They move into the bedroom and Dean grabs some of his comfier clothes and lays them out on the bed for Phoebe, then quickly departs, leaving her to get dressed in peace. Rejection crashes into Phoebe and she lets out a gasp as a flashback takes her by surprise.

Joel grabs a fist of Phoebe's hair, pulling it tightly and Phoebe lets out a scream of pain, her bound hands trying to pull his hands away from her head. Nausea floods her and she pukes on the floor in front of them, but Joel pays it no mind, pulling her through it and her stomach rolls as regurgitated food sticks to her skin. But what she sees in front of her makes her whimper and digs her heels into the ground below her. Joel lets out a grunt and forces her forward further, pulling her to a stop in front of what can only be described as a coffin, but it's stood up on its end, the height the exact same for Phoebe when she is kneeling.

"No Joel, please, not again." She screams but Joel ignores her, tying a scarf around her mouth, effectively shutting her up before turning her around and shoving her backwards into the coffin. She lets out a muffled scream as Joel slams the door, a little window open at her eyeline, Joel squatting down in front of it, his dark eyes swirling in anger.

"You will stay here for the next day or two, no food, no water, nothing until you can learn to accept your role in my life. You really never should have agreed to move in with me, mummy and daddy might still be alive." He says maliciously and Phoebe screams in

rage at him, banging on the front of the coffin with her bound hands. Joel squints at her dangerously and moves away from the little window, locking the door of the coffin with a thick chain. Phoebe whimpers, knowing that even as she's locked in her, she isn't safe from his ruthless punishment. Panic floods her brain as the darkness creeps around her, teasing her with the unknown as she can't look behind her or above her. Quick as lightning, Joel opens the topside of the coffin and pours something over her head. Hundreds of little legs cover Phoebe's body and she screams in terror as she feels a spider crawl across her face. She thrashes in the coffin, trying to escape, but the chains around it hold steady, and Joel watches from the outside with evil glee. He moves to behind the coffin, and opens a secret backdoor, one level with Phoebe's behind and lower regions. Phoebe doesn't hear him open it as she screams hysterically but she jumps when she feels something hard run up the backs of her legs. A gentle prod at her entrance has her crying out in fear and she tries to clamp her legs shut but to no avail, and she screams as Joel thrusts a dildo into her forcefully, it grating against her walls and she howls in pain from behind the makeshift gag. Joel pulls down a hook from the ceiling and attaches it to the chains, before pressing a button and the coffin raises from the floor of the basement. Phoebe's stomach clenches as she feels the coffin sway in mid-air, and she lets out another scream as more spiders thread themselves into her hair. Joel laughs hysterically from behind her (she thinks), and tilts the coffin so it is laying as it would in a grave. He presses the dildo further into her entrance before removing it quickly and shoving it into her puckered rear and she screams again, tears soaking the make shift gag and she thrashes continually. Joel slams his fist on the coffin and Phoebe stills instantly, scared for what's going to happen next. Joel forces the dildo to stay inside her as he forces himself into her entrance, thrusting viciously and determinedly, Phoebe sobs quietly, trying not to move as pain rushes through her body, as if she is being split into.

Phoebe lets out a gasp as her brain lets her free from her memories, and she leans against the bedroom wall with a shaky hand before composing herself. She grabs the clothes Dean laid out for her and quickly pulls them on before attempting to tame her wild hair, before giving up and joining Dean in the kitchen. Dean doesn't say anything as he takes in her appearance and gently nudges out a stool with his foot.

Chapter Seven

Phoebe and Dean sit at the counter in his apartment, laughing at each other's jokes and just flirting. Phoebe blushes as his hand brushes with hers briefly but he pulls it back quickly, before glancing away from her. Confusion etches her face and a fist tightens around her heart.

"Did I do something wrong?" she asks.

"No Squidge, you haven't done anything wrong, it's my own fucked up head." He says with a sigh as he runs his hands through his hair in frustration before rolling his shoulders slightly. She gets up to walk around the counter and starts pulling things out of the fridge and Dean looks at her in curiosity.

"What are you doing Squidge?"

"Well, you always take care of me and listen to all my shit, now it's my turn," she explains as she cuts up a cucumber and puts it in a bowl, before wiping down the surface with some kitchen roll and then beginning to cut up a pepper, staring at in intently.

"I don't want to burden you with any of my stuff when you have your own things to deal with," he mutters, putting his head in his hands before looking back up at her.

"Alright, none of that Dean," she says, waving the knife around a tad for dramatic effect, "you have helped me so much, the least I can do it listen to what you say and offer as much support as I can."

"I don't really know what to say to be honest, I normally only talk about these things with my therapist, but she's always batting her eyes at me to try and help properly. I mean she does help, and I'm defiantly a lot better from going to therapy but there's so much more work to be done." His eyes flick down to where Phoebe is gripping the knife tightly as she slices through a piece of pepper harshly at the mention of the therapist eyeing her man. *Her man*, she thinks, *he's not my man, no matter how much I want him to be. It's not safe.*

"I think your therapist would probably suggest talking to others as well, not about everything but sharing some of the things will make it easier for you to deal with and allow others to support you," she jumps as Dean pins her with an incredulous look, "I know, it's like calling the pot kettle but that's different." Dean rolls his eyes but starts to speak again, softly, to the point that Phoebe stops cutting the pepper to listen to him.

"When I was a kid, I didn't have this amazing upbringing that the rest of my friends did. My dad was a drunk and would hit me and my brother whenever we did something as much as breathed on him wrong. My mum was so hopped on pain meds and anti-depressants that she became this... shell of a person... like she was there but not really there. When I was eleven, my dad was being particularly vicious one day, he was calling my mum every name under the sun and would beat her to an inch of her life. I lost count how many times we went to the ER." He looks at Phoebe quickly before looking down at his hands resting on the countertop, when Phoebe squints her eyes and can see tiny scars and discolouration mapping his flawless skin. He sees where she is looking and quickly puts his hands in his lap before clearing his throat and continuing.

"On that day, is when I lost both my brother and my mum. My dad hit my mum over the head with a vase upstairs and when my brother rushed to help her, my dad kicked him down the stairs, breaking his neck."

"Where you were all in this?"

"As soon as my dad started yelling, I hid in the laundry basket. I'd smelled the whiskey on his breath earlier that afternoon and knew it wasn't going to be a good day. When he got like that, all three of us had so many spaces to his around the house that we could mostly wait until he passed out in his own piss and vomit." He shook his head and guilt wraps around his body tightly, constricting his lungs and forcing him to take a deep breath in.

"It wasn't your fault, you were just a child, there was nothing you could have done," she says gently, not wanting to offend him or say the wrong thing. He laughs humourlessly.

"I wish it was me sometimes that had died instead of my brother, my father blamed me for his death, saying that I should have held him back." Phoebe's eyes widen in disbelief and she puts the knife down slowly.

"What did you do after that happened? Surely the cops came looking?"

"I grew up a while away from here Squidge, it was different. I wasn't born into the life I have now, I had to work my ass off to get here. Back where I'm from, everyone kept out of everyone's business, even if there were kids and women involved. That's why I built this company, to protect those who can't defend themselves. I never want anyone to be in the position I was in."

"That's very admirable Dean, but you do know you won't be able to help everyone right?"

"I know that but with this company I have saved over 15,000 women and children from abusive partners, giving them homes and a support system. I do also do some darker stuff but I am not sure if you are ready for that just yet." Dean says, with a coy smile playing on his lips, pride blooming in his chest.

"What do you do Dean? If we want to be together, then I need to know details. I can't do secrecy, not again."

"Me and my team get rid of the abusive partners...", he says, not meeting Phoebe's eyes.

"You kill them?" she queries, no fear lacing her words as she asks him.

"Yes."

"Good." Dean flicks his eyes to meet hers, raising an eyebrow. He looks over her form, trying to detect any dishonesty but finding none. Phoebe rolls her shoulders back and goes back to trying to cut the pepper.

She reads the note with a shaky breath; "I'm not sure how I feel about literal murder but part of me is happy that those scum bags never walk the earth again," she states, aggressively slicing the pepper and Dean watches her with a slight hint of fear. He slowly stands up and walks round to Phoebe, careful not startle her, and reaching down to take the knife out of her hands.

"I think it's safe to say that we have both been dealt crappy cards throughout our lives, but it's what we do with the rest of our lives that count."

"I didn't think I'd ever get out of the life I was trapped in, so I have no clue what I want to do. I love working at the coffee shop but I have working for my boss." She says with huff, sighing as the knife is carefully placed down on the side. Dean smirks and shakes his head before ordering pizza on his phone.

"That's for you to figure out Squidge, I'll support you no matter what you want to do, and it doesn't matter how long it takes for you to figure it out. In the meantime, would you like me to book you an appointment with a therapist? I could try a new one for you or you can speak to the one I do. Of course, there is patient confidentiality so you wouldn't need to worry about someone finding out what you said in those sessions." Dean grabs two cups from the cupboard, the stoppers allowing the cupboard not to slam as Dean shuts it with a bit more force than necessary.

"I'll give it a go. I haven't seen one before, I've just kind of battled on," Dean pins her with a disapproving look, "oh don't look at me like that. Between me pulling extra shifts at work and running away from my psycho ex, I didn't really have time to stop and process what's happened to me and why."

"I'll try and get you booked in the next few days. The woman is very busy but I'm sure I can work my magic and get you squeezed in." Dean says, batting his eyes at Phoebe, a small laugh falling from her lips and Dean looks at them gently. Her tongue licks her lips, soothing the small patch of dry skin then appeared out of nowhere. Dean follows the movement and inches a tiny bit in front of her, looking at her for permission. She nods slowly, heart thumping in both their chests as Dean runs a knuckle along her cheek. Phoebe closes her eyes and allows herself to lean into his touch, and he bends down slowly, softly running his lips along hers as she lets out a small gasp. His hand gently cradles the back of her head and his lips meet hers in a small sign of desperation. She moans against his mouth and kisses him back, teeth clashing together as they let themselves both feel the tension coming off one another. Phoebe giggles softly and Dean pulls back in confusion.

"I didn't realise this was a laughing matter?" he asks playfully, his hand still resting on the back of her head.

"I just never thought I'd be in your apartment, let alone kissing you in it." Phoebe says honestly. She bumps her nose against Dean's, before brushing her lips against his again then pulling away. She slowly grabs his hand, checking his face for any sign of distress or regret, and when she finds none, she pulls him towards the bedroom. His eyes flash in surprise.

"Oh no Mr, nothing like that, but it's getting late and I'm tired so cuddles?" Dean nods quickly and follows her to his bedroom, still holding her hand but loosens his grip when he feels a slight tremor. The two of the clamber in his bed and Phoebe starts to build a little pillow wall.

"What's that for?"

"Well I want to sleep next to you, but I don't want to accidentally beat you up in my sleep when I have a nightmare so... precautions," Phoebe states as she adjusts the pillows higher, hooking a leg up and checking it's high enough that she won't hit Dean with her flailing limbs. He looks at her with a blank stare before shrugging and getting in on his side of the bed.

"Whatever helps you sleep at night Squidge, although I was promised cuddles."

"I underestimated how tired I actually was, and I feel like I could pass out any second Dean, we can have cuddles in the morning." Phoebe sets the pillows her head will be on at the right angle, before shimmying under the covers and closing her eyes gently.

"It's probably a good thing you are tired anyway, since we are getting up early to continue your training and then I am taking you out properly."

"Out where?" Phoebe asks hesitantly, still very much aware that Joel is still looking for her.

"I am taking you out during the day, I'm not telling you where just yet but just know you'll love it Squidge," he says as his voice grows softer with sleep creeping in. For the first time in years, Phoebe falls asleep with a smile on her face.

Chapter Eight

Exhaustion fills Phoebe's eyes as she pries them open at the sound of the door opening. For a moment she forgets where she is, until Dean's voice floods the place as he perches on the end of the bed.

"Squidge? You awake?" She lets out a grunt in protest and pulls the soft linen over her eyes, hearing him chuckle at the movement. Her hands fist at the sheets as she tries to prevent Dean from pulling them off but to no avail. With one hard yank he pulls them off of her and stands there with a massive grin that makes his eyes twinkle in the early morning sun.

"Come on Squidge, up and at 'em. You wanted to start training to defend yourself, so early morning starts are a must." Phoebe groans and blinks up at him in mock anger before begrudgingly getting out of the comfy bed. She picks up the clothes that Dean has laid out for her, a dark green crop top and some black shorts before chucking them on and slipping into her trainers. Dean gives her a once over before nodding and heading out the door.

As they walk through the kitchen, Dean grabs himself and Phoebe a protein shake to drink as they take the elevator down to the bottom floor.

"What are we going to be focusing on today?" Phoebe asks after she takes a sip of the shake, turning her nose up as the banana flavour overwhelms her tastebuds. Dean lets out a small chuckle as he watches her try to stomach the foul tasting drink.

"Would you like mine instead? It's chocolate flavoured? And in response to your question, I thought we could run through a more manoeuvre's after we've warmed up, and then potentially move on to you using a knife to defend yourself?" He looks over at her and leans against the elevator door, trying to read how she feels. Phoebe keeps a blank expression and nods absentmindedly, before shaking her head and coming back into the present.

"Could I try some of yours please? I'm sorry I don't like this one, but I just can't stomach bananas."

Dean smiles at her before swapping her drink with his and watches in satisfaction as she lets out a happy sigh. She then looks at him curiously.

"Why are you helping me?"

"What do you mean?", a puzzled expression forming on his face and his eyebrows furrowing.

"Well, when I started opening up to you, you could have left me. And after you saw my PTSD attack the other night, you could have never messaged me again. So why are you helping me?"

"Isn't it obvious Phoebe?" when she shakes her head, he continues with a sigh, "because I knew that underneath all that trauma and pain, there is a girl that wants to be desperately loved the right way. Someone who despite everything you have been through, loves so hard and ferociously, and I guess I just wanted to get to know you, and I have found it so easy to… adore you." An awkward silence floods the elevator and Phoebe shuffles her feet, whilst looking anywhere but Dean.

"You don't have to say anything back, but you asked and that's my answer." The elevator doors open with a ping and they both step out into reception of the apartment before walking through the heavy doors to the gym. They set their shakes down on a bench in the corner and head to the treadmill to warm up. Phoebe and Dean walk at a brisk pace, but not wanting to overdo it like last time. Dean links his phone to the speakers and passes it over to Phoebe silently. She grabs it with a shaking hand and puts on a bassy song, flooding the gym with electric guitars and drums. Dean bobs his head in time with the music and turns up the speed of the treadmills a bit. Phoebe puffs a bit but manages to keep up. Before long, they are both covered in sweat and they jump off the machines, the music still playing as they head over to the sparring mats.

"Let's go through the stances and moves again, and if you're feeling confident we can move onto practicing with a knife." She nods but still refuses to look at him. Dean eyes her warily before dropping into an offensive position. Phoebe rolls her shoulders, taking a deep breath and the focusing on Dean and how he's positioned his feet. His weight leans more onto his left and when he dashes at her, she twists out of his grip and kicks at his right leg before landing a solid blow to his ribs. He grits his teeth but lets out a small smile before stepping back.

"Good. Let's go again but we aren't going to stop until one of us is pinned, okay?" He says as he wipes away sweat covering his forehead.

"Don't go easy on me. You wanted to train me, so let's do this." They dodge each other's attacks for a few minutes before Phoebe swipes her leg underneath Dean's, causing him to tumble to the ground with a thump. She rushes on top of him and pins his hands down with her knees, using a bit of force as he struggles underneath her. She smiles victoriously at him, and Dean's heart clenches in happiness at the look on her face. He then flips them with a quick buck of his hips so she is lying underneath him. A flash of panic overcomes Phoebe but she quickly pushes it away, knowing she is safe. Dean smirks and goes to give her a peck on the cheek, but she turns her head at the last minute and their mouths meet in a blazing kiss. Dean stops suddenly and gives her a questioning look, waiting for her approval. When she nods back with a small smile, he kisses her with so much passion that Phoebe forgets how to breath and her eyes flutter closed as her fingers wrap around his shoulders as she kisses him back. Dean's tongue swipes at her lips, and she opens without hesitation. Their tongues battle for dominance, and Dean eventually submits, letting Phoebe explore him. Her hands run up his shirt and her fingers gently map the contours of his abs and muscles. Dean lets out a soft groan into her mouth and nudges her legs open with his knee. He feels the warm heat from her over his knee and he grinds it ever so slightly into her core. She stops moving for a second before rolling her hip and letting out a small whimper as pleasure races through her body. But before they can go any further, the doors of the gym burst open, the hour they had blocked off for their training over. Dean groans in annoyance but untangles himself from Phoebe's hold, as she lays there, panting softly before brushing the hair out of her face. Dean smiles at her flustered expression before offering his hand and pulling her to her feet, causing her to stumble a bit. He grabs her arm to steady her before looking at the man entering the gym with so much anger, the tension in the gym so thick it could be cut with a knife. Phoebe drops her head in embarrassment at them being caught making out like a pair of horny teenagers, and they walk to the elevator in silence.

As they select the button to Dean's floor, he pushes her gently against the wall, looking at her for any hesitation. When he sees none, he kisses her again, nipping at her lip as she lets out a small gasp. His hands rest on her hips and her top rises up as he feels her skin beneath his hands, the smoothness in contrast with the roughness of her scars as he traces them absentmindedly. Their teeth clash and soft moans flood the space; the only reason they stop is when the elevator doors open and they pull away breathless. Deans hand holds hers gently as they step put into his apartment.

"Go have a shower Squidge, and then I'm taking you out."

"Where are we going? Also I have none of my clothes."

"Now that would be telling, it's a surprise. Also I had Jessica drop off most of your clothes last night whilst you were asleep. They should all be hung up in the wardrobe." He beams at her and heads towards the kitchen, moving to make coffees for the drive and to fix up some snacks. Phoebe moves to the bedroom and quickly jumps in the shower, not wanting to keep Dean waiting. Once she has cleaned and shaved everywhere, she pads across the bedroom to the wardrobe and opens the door, finding all her clothes arranged in occasion and style. She rolls her eyes and smiles, knowing that Dean was the one to organise this. The sun beams into the bedroom and it warms her skin gently. She quickly dries her hair and lets a few strands frame her face. Phoebe pulls out a red skater dress, with flowers all around the bottom. She looks at it sceptically before shrugging and pulling it on. The soft fabric falls graciously against her skin and Phoebe pulls out a white denim jacket from the wardrobe, putting it on the bed as she hears Dean walking towards the bedroom. The door opens slowly and he pokes his head in, as she moves to hunt for some white socks.

"Can I come in? Also socks are in the bedside table, second drawer down."

"Yes of course, it's your bedroom Dean." She says as she grabs some socks and pulls them over her feet, teetering as she tries to balance on one foot, then the other.

"It's as much yours as is mine. Are you almost ready?" he asks as he steps into the bedroom. His words falter at the last word, as his eyes grow wide, taking in Phoebe's appearance.

"Is everything okay? Should I change? Do my scars make you uncomfortable? I'm showing too much skin aren't I?" she fires multiple questions at him, anxiety coursing through her veins as her hands begin to shake. Dean walks over and grabs her hands in one hand, before gripping her chin gently and tilting her face to meet his.

"Okay, first of all, there is no problem. You shouldn't change, no your scars don't make me uncomfortable, and you are not showing too much skin. If you want to wear the dress, I'm not complaining, I think you look absolutely stunning." Phoebe searches his face for any trace of dishonesty and she nods despite the gentle grip Dean still has on her chin. He gives her a quick peck on the cheek and releases her chin. A blush creeps up her face and she clears her throat.

"Are you going to jump in the shower before we leave?"

"Yes, I'm going to get in now, so we should be leaving in the next twenty minutes, if that's okay." She nods and watches as he retreats to the bathroom. Once she hears the water running, she starts rummaging for a pair of shoes, finding her old trusty white vans and slipping them onto her feet. She sits on the bed as she waits for Dean to finish in the shower, humming to herself and swaying her feet a little. Dean comes out of the shower a few minutes later, a towel wrapped around his waist whilst he uses another to dry his fluffy hair. Dean's eyes twinkle with mischief and he goes to move the towel around his waist. Phoebe lets out a little squeak and clamps her eyes closed, heart beating erratically. Dean lets out a soft chuckle before quickly drying the rest of his body before pulling on his underwear and grabbing a white shirt from one of his drawers, yanking it over his head and then grabbing some shorts from another drawer. After he's done getting dressed, he walks over to Phoebe and gives her a kiss on the head. She peeps one eye open tentatively, seeing that Dean is now fully clothed and opens the other eye. Dean steps between her swinging legs and gives her a peck on the lips before grabbing her jacket and handing it to her. He swiftly puts on some black trainers and then grabs Phoebes hand, his shaking a bit. Phoebe giggles and pulls him to the kitchen and they each grab their hot drinks and Phoebe hoists her bag from the side onto her shoulder before they make their way down to Dean's car.

Dean opens the door for Phoebe and she slides easily into the seat, clipping the belt in place and Dean walks round to the driver's seat. They put their drinks in the cup holders before looking at each other, a moment passes before they burst out laughing.

"This is a bit awkward isn't it?" Dean says as he puts the key in the ignition and turns the car on. Phoebe lets out a chuckle and nods.

"I don't really know what to do after an act of intimacy or affection. I'm not used to it so I don't know how to handle the situation", she speaks through little giggles, "also, are you now going to tell me where we are going?"

"I think we both just need to try and be ourselves. Also, nope, you'll find out when we get there, just know that I know you'll have a great time."

"You've been talking to Jessica haven't you?"

"Maybe." Dean turns the corners easily, hand resting gently on Phoebe's thigh. They fall into a comfortable silence as Dean drives them to the mystery location. Phoebe sips her chai latter and watches as the trees race past the windows. As Dean turns off onto a beaten road, a sign appears saying 'Aquarium This Way'. She lets out an excited squeal and turns to Dean with excited eyes, looking at him in disbelief. A broad grin creeps up Deans face and he looks at her out of the corner of his eye.

"Yep, we are going to the aquarium. Jessica said you have never been and you are obsessed with starfish, so I thought what better to see one up close rather than driving for four hours to the beach." He explains, as he pulls into a parking space, popping the car in neutral and applying the handbrake. He pulls out the tickets from the glove box and hands them to Phoebe. Her fingers brush against his gently as she takes the tickets to look at them, but when she does, another ticket falls out into her lap. In bold letters, the ticket says;

Ticket for one person for the starfish pool experience.

Phoebe lets out a tiny scream and throws herself across the centre console, wrapping her arms around Dean's chest and nuzzling into his neck. He lets out a chesty laugh and runs his hands over her shoulders, giving them a gentle squeeze before dropping a kiss on the top of her head.

"I'm guessing I did good?", he murmurs in her ear, and he feels her nod against his chest. He slowly pulls her away and opens his door. As he walks around the car, Pheobe gathers her things and remembers to grab their drinks. Her door opens and Dean extends his hand to her, which she grabs slowly and allows him to pull her out the car graciously. The rough stones hurt her feet through the shoes but they walk hand in hand to the entrance of the aquarium. The gentle breeze flows through both of their hairs, and Dean pushes the door open as they make their way inside. Dean nods at the staff members behind the counter and they open one of the other doors before following them into the aquarium. Soft blue lights flood the space as they seem to step into another world. All different kinds of jellyfish line along one side of the walls, whilst on the other small fishes bob through the water. Phoebe looks around in amazement and Dean eyes her with adoration. They stay hand in hand as they walk around together, Phoebe rambling random facts about every aquatic creature they see, Dean listening intently. Her face turns red as she realises she's rambling and she mutters a small 'sorry', before attempting to let go of Dean's hand. He holds fast and spins her to look at him.

"Never apologise for being passionate about something Squidge, it's one of my favourite things, listening to you 'ramble'." He kisses her slowly, mapping out her mouth and then the worker leads them to rock pool in a side room. There are a few people stood around, a mother with her kids, an old couple, a group of men huddled near the entrances and exits, and a man in the corner with a cap on, staring intently at the pool. Phoebe gasps and shuffles over to the pool, eyes beaming wide as she looks into the clear water. Below the surface, ten or so different coloured starfish cling to rocks, tentacles swaying slightly from the water. Pheobe rests her hands on the side of the pool and waves Dean over. He walks slowly over, and rests his hand on her lower back, resting his chin on the top of her head. She giggles softly and listens as the worker asks questions about starfish, which Phoebe answers rapidly, blushing furiously as they stare at her with disbelief.

"Okay, since you know so much about starfish, I'm going to ask you a question, and if you get it right, you can have anything from the giftshop for free." The worker says with a soft smile, eyes twinkling as Phoebe nods.

"How do starfish eat their food?" Phoebe turns to look at the mother and her kids and beckons them over. She whispers something to the kids before speaking.

"I'm not sure on that one but I think the kids here know." The mothers face lights up and she nudges the kids forward to speak. Their faces light up and they speak confidently

"They have tiny suction cups they use to hold onto their food", they turn to look at Phoebe and she nods before they start speaking again "when they eat, their stomachs get out of their body and eat the food, but then goes back in when they have finished." The worker smiles and nods at Phoebe before turning to the children and beaming at them.

"Well done, that's correct although I'm surprised you knew that. I'll speak to my coworkers and make sure they know you both get a free gift at the shop." The children squeal and run back to their mother. Dean presses on her back again and Phoebe turns to look at him. Happiness shines through his eyes and he gives her a quick peck on the cheek. Shivers run along her body, and goosebumps rise in their wake. The feeling of being watched rushes over the both of them, and they turn the heads around the room. No one stands out of the ordinary but the group of men keep an eye on the man in the corner. Phoebe bristles slightly as she realises its Dean's guards hiding in plain sight but doesn't say anything. The worker beckons Phoebe over to where they are standing, ushering her behind the gated area. Phoebe hums with excitement and listens as the worker tells her the correct way to touch the starfish. She practically vibrates with anticipation and she looks over at Dean, catching him already looking at her with so much love that it makes her chest ache. Tears form in the corner of her eyes, and she quickly blinks them away as she runs her finger over the bumpy skin of the starfish. She lets out a soft giggle as the arm of the sea creature moves a bit, but she can't help it as goosebumps rise along her arms. Her breath catches in her chest but she shakes her head gently and looks back at Dean. His eyes have narrowed and his gaze is trained on the man wearing a baseball cap. Not wanting the creep to spoil the day, Phoebe steps back from the pool after thanking the assistant before she walks over to Dean. His eyes shift to her and they soften slightly, his hand reaching out to her. She takes it without a second thought and they make their way to the doors, waiting for his guards to open them.

They step through the doors and into the twisting tunnels below the biggest fishtank in the aquarium. Soft blue lights flood the space and all kinds of aquatic creatures swim above their heads. They stay silent as they both admire the shark swimming in circles, like it's chasing its own tail. The black tips of its fins stand out against the soft greys of its body. Dean's thumb gently runs over Phoebe's hand and she gently squeezes it in return. He quickly looks around before ushering her over to a wide pillar off the side of the tunnel. Phoebe lets out a squeak of surprise but doesn't try and stop him. He pushes her against the pillar, caging her in before staring intently at her. She nods slowly, a smile creeping up her face along with a red tint flooding her cheeks. Dean lets out a soft chuckle before his lips meet her with a sense of urgency, teeth clashing and noses bumping as Phoebe lets out a soft whimper. He slows down a bit, letting her run her hands along his arms, groaning gently at the contact. His knee nudges in between her legs, causing the dress to slide up a bit. Phoebe lets out a gasp in shock and very slowly, moves her hips on his knee. She lets out a little moan and Dean pins her with a look before leaning down to whisper in her ear.

"I'm going to need you to be quite for me Squidge, we don't want to get kicked out do we?", he says teasingly as he softly nips at her neck and ear. She shakes her head quickly, eliciting a chuckle from him. His hands run over her sides as he removes his knee from in between her thighs. Phoebe whines in protest, but his hand quickly replaces where his knee was, her lips forming a soft 'o' as she realises what he is doing. His fingers dance along the waistband of her underwear, edging under but not moving to where she needs him most. He watches her face, feeling awe at the way her hips buck towards him and she clamps her mouth shut. Sweat runs along her hairline, and her hands grasp onto his shoulders for support. He finally eases a finger under her underwear and strokes at her clit gently, his eyes never leaving hers, trying to find any distress. When he finds none, he dips the tip of his finger into her, watching as she struggles to stay quiet as her eyes fly open, meeting his gaze. She lifts up her leg, wrapping it around his waist and dragging him closer. His free hand comes up and pushes on her chest slightly, pinning her in place before he dips more of his finger in. She whimpers softly before Dean feels her walls clamping down on his finger. He groans softly at her grip and strokes her gently, his breath coming out in tiny gasps as well. Phoebe lets out a shudder and a gasp, attempting to bury her face in his neck, but the force on her chest holds fast as Dean just watches her intently. She whimpers and bucks against his finger before her head falls back, chest heaving and face flushing. Phoebe taps at his shoulder and Dean slowly removes his finger before wiping it on a cloth in his pocket. He helps her sort her dress out before draping his arm over her shoulder and kissing her on the top of her head. They stand in silence for a minute, both computing what had just happened, before Phoebe starts talking about some of the things in the tank. Dean's guards stand nearby, and a camera flash briefly illuminates the area. Phoebe lets out a gasp in shock, and watches as the aquarium staff, grab the man wearing a baseball cap and escort him to the door, whilst pointing at the sign clearly stating that flash photography isn't allowed.

"I wasn't taking pictures of the fish. I was taking photos of him and her", he shouts whilst pointing at both Dean and Phoebe, anger on his face but he refuses to meet Phoebe's gaze. The attendant rolls their eyes and ushers the man out, apologising for the commotion and slamming the door behind them and the man. Dean pulls her into his side protectively and breathes in her scent as he tries to contain the anger bubbling under his skin. As she turns and puts her face in his chest, Dean glares at Jack and Leon before nodding his head to the way the man got escorted out. They nod back, like robots, and walk after him.

"Shall we go home Squidge or would you like to stay?", he murmurs in her ear softly, not wanting to startle her.

"I don't want to go home yet but I don't want to stay. Can we get food please?", she asks, looking up at him with tears in her eyes, a few escaping onto her cheeks. Dean nods and rubs the pads of his thumbs over the tears, wiping her skin free. She wraps her arms around him and buries her face in his chest, nuzzling in gently. He bends down and kisses the top off her head before gently pulling her away from his embrace and grabbing her hand delicately. They slowly start walking out the aquarium, Dean asking about some of the fishes to get Phoebe distracted from the situation. Her eyes glaze over and her hands begin to shake. Dean grabs both of her hands in one of his and moves her over to a corner. Her breathing becomes erratic and she looks at Dean with tear filled eyes. Dean holds her gaze, running his thumbs over her hands as he whispers, "you're okay, that man can't hurt you, he's been escorted out and my guards will deal with him."

"If they can find him." She says breathlessly.

"What do you mean?"

"I'm like, ninety percent sure that it was Joel, although I didn't see his face", she lets out a gasp and bursts into tears, "I thought I had escaped him but he always finds me." Dean's heart hammers at the thought of Joel finding Phoebe, instinctively he asks,

"Move in with me?", the question shocking Phoebe out of her distressed state. Her head flies back to stare at Dean, eyes wide and eyebrows up to her hairline. A few wisps fall into her face and she brushes them away aggressively, searching Dean's face for any ulterior motive. When she finds nothing but honesty on his face, she slowly nods.

"Good, I have a lot of security in that building and no one can get in unless they live there. I can have some of my men pick up your stuff, is there anything you desperately need?"

She nods but before speaking, Dean starts ushering them both to the exit and to the car. Dean opens the door and Phoebe slides into the seat, her back slumping against the plush leather seats. Dean opens the glove box and hands her a notepad and pen, before getting into the driver's seat.

"Write down anything you'll need. Don't worry how big or small it is, I'll make sure my men get it. Whilst we are out, would you like to go shopping for some food that you'll like?" Phoebe nods again and starts writing on the notepad, Dean glancing over her shoulder as she writes.

"Are you going to need any female products?", he asks as he puts the key in the ignition and starts the engine, easing out of the parking space and onto the main road.

"I should be fine, since going on the pill, I haven't had any periods in a few years. But it probably wouldn't be a bad idea to get some on the off chance? Have you got a box or anything that I can hide them in?"

"Hide them? Why would you want to hide them?" Dean turns to look at her, disbelief flooding his face. Heat creeps up her face and she looks away from Dean's intense gaze.

"I've always been told to keep that... stuff locked away, that no one would want to see it."

"Let me guess, by that piece of shit that is your ex-boyfriend?" Dean's grip tightens on the steering wheel, the leather creaking slightly under the pressure. Phoebe's eyes flit down to look at it but doesn't say anything. She shrugs in response to his question, gently bouncing the pen off the notebook and looks out the window. Sensing her shutting down, Dean hastily changes the topic.

"So what kind of food do you want to get?"

"Hmm, I'm not sure, I don't eat that much, only when Jessica is around. There's certain things I eat but I don't actually like them."

"Why do you eat them then?", he asks, slightly scared of the answer.

"When I was dating Joel, if I didn't eat the food he wanted then I wouldn't eat. I guess maybe I'm still stuck in that way of thinking." Dean takes a deep breath before speaking.

"Okay, we need to find you some food that you like, I don't care if I have to buy the shop." Phoebe turns to look at him, blinking slowly. He looks at her out the corner of his eye, a small smile coming onto his face.

"What? This may come as a slight shock, judging by the look on your face, but this is how two people in relationship are supposed to treat each other. Respect, honesty and trustworthy." Phoebe blinks twice before shaking her head.

"Nope, nada, zilch. That's not how relationships work Dean". He lets out a deep chuckle and nods as she continues to shake her head. He flips the indicator on and pulls into a supermarket, killing the engine and getting out of the car. As he walks round to Phoebe's side, she calms her breathing and the pounding in her chest, mulling over the fact that he just called what they had a 'relationship'. Dean opens the door and sticks his head in, his lips brushing her ear.

"Yes I did just say we are in a relationship, now get out of the car and we will find some food you like. I don't care how long it takes." Phoebe quickly unplugs her seatbelt and grabs his hand, allowing him to pull her out the car. They walk hand in hand to the store and Phoebe makes a move to grab a trolley. Dean stares at her before grabbing the trolley himself, and pointing to her to stand near him.

"We are shopping for you Squidge, so you need to be the one to pick out food." He gently nudges her in front of the trolley and Phoebe grabs it tightly as they start walking around the store. Every time she goes to pick something up, she glances at Dean, seeking approval and he nods slightly, his lips tight as he tries to get her to think of herself. As they walk past the snack aisle, Phoebe stops and stares at the selection, eyes roaming over the assortment of crisps, chocolates and sweets. She shrugs and moves on, Dean falling behind to grab the items she stared at the longest. He places them below a few things in the trolley, hiding them from view. They near the end of the store and start placing things on the conveyer belt. When Phoebe notices the snacks, her hand stops mid-air. Dean loads them onto the belt and Phoebe grabs them, putting them back in the trolley.

"What are you doing Squidge?"

"I'm not allowed snacks," she says bluntly.

"What do you mean?", Dean says as he puts the snacks back on the belt, ignoring the look from the cashier.

"That's exactly what I mean. I'm not allowed snacks." She gives him a small glare and he sighs in defeat, not wanting to push her too much. He unloads the snacks and places them back in the trolley, before whipping out his phone and messaging Jack.

"Okay if you're sure. I'll get Jack to buy them because I feel a bit awkward handing them over to the cashier to put them back on the shelf." She nods and starts bagging up the food that's already been processed through the tills. Dean helps her load up the bags and taps his card on the reader and they slowly walk back to the car after thanking the cashier.

"Are we going to talk about what happened in there?", he says as he loads the bags into the boot of the car.

"Nope, I really don't want to talk about it," Phoebe states as she helps load some things into the car before grabbing the trolley and taking it back to where they grabbed it. Dean sighs softly as he watches her retreating form, before grabbing his phone from his pocket and ringing one of his staff members.

"Archie? Have you found anything on Joel?", his voice tense as he watches Phoebe struggle to put the key in the trolley.

"No Sir, nothing yet. Whoever this Joel character is, he's good at covering his tracks, but I'm better, I just need a bit more time to find him. I can assure though, I will find him." Archies voice pounds in Dean's head, his vision turning red slightly but quickly bottling it down as Phoebe walks back over, running her hands through her hair and brushing off her dress.

"I know you will Archie, but please hurry. I want to get rid of this fucker, he's hurt Phoebe for too long."

"I know Sir, and I'll work on it. Phoebe's a sweet girl; despite everything she's been through." Dean nods even though Archie can't see him and hangs up the phone, before looking at Phoebe. She stares down at her shoes, shuffling them in the ground and tapping her hands on her thighs.

"I'm sorry", she whispers.

"It's okay Squidge, I just want what's best for you, but if this is too much too soon, then we can always slow down." She shakes her head.

"I don't want to slow down. I'm just scared you're going to realise that I'm too much hassle."

"Never going to happen", Dean says as he gives her a kiss on the forehead and helps her into the passenger seat. They drive back to the flat in comfortable silence, both of them mulling over the events of the day in their heads.

Chapter Nine

Phoebe and Dean walk to the flat, both of them carrying bags of food from their shopping trip. Phoebe places her bags on the counter and begins to unpack them, before realising there is nowhere to put them. Dean lets out a soft chuckle as he brings up the rear, putting his bags on the floor, then walking to kiss Phoebe on the head.

"What's wrong Squidge?"

"I don't know where to put all the food we got?", she scratches at her head, turning round to face Dean, an amused look on his face as he stares down at her. Phoebe pins him with a look before speaking.

"Well I don't know, do I? I have only been here a handful of times, so I don't want to intrude on your space."

"What did you think me asking you to move in meant?", a small smirk creeping up his mouth, his eyes twinkling with mischief.

"Err..."

"It means that what's mine is yours. This space is yours. You want a reading chair? Consider it done. You want to paint the walls bright pink? We can talk about it. You want a snack basket in the bedroom or an emergency room? Done and done. I want you to be happy here Squidge, and I want you to be safe." Dean's hands move to Phoebe's waist, resting gently as he looks down at her with so much earnest, that it makes her heart thump erratically in her chest. Her hands run up his arms, feeling his muscles tighten slightly at her touch before relaxing slightly. Phoebe tilts her head up slightly, brushing her lips along Dean's. Het lets out a groan before releasing her.

"If that's on the table, then we need to get this food packed away before it goes bad." Phoebe hums but keeps a hand on his arm for a few seconds, relishing in the fact that she doesn't feel scared to touch him. Together they move as a unit, putting food in the cupboards, Dean offering advice to where things should go. Phoebe moves around happily, seemingly gliding over the floor. Dean takes a step back and watches as she finds herself in his space, well now theirs. Anticipation courses through his veins at the thought of having Phoebe here most of the time. He grabs the piece of paper off the counter that has the list of things Phoebe would like from her flat, and he texts Jessica a photo of the list. He locks the phone and puts it face down on the counter. Phoebe looks at him then the phone, then him again.

"Why have you put it face down like that?"

"What do you mean?" Dean's brows furrowing in confusion.

"Whenever Joel did that, it was either to hide something or someone. So I'll ask again, why did you put your phone down like that?" Phoebe crosses her arms over her chest and Dean takes a deep breath before slowly moving over to her. He looks around at the kitchen, seeing everything is out away before speaking, slight irritation in his voice.

"I am not hiding anything. I just texted Jessica to bring some of the things from your flat that you asked for. I am not going to let you see my phone, because that would be a violation of your trust in me, but you'll know I'm telling the truth when Jessica turns up later."

"So you weren't texting another woman about meeting up later or something whilst I am asleep?" Phoebe's eyes never leave Dean's and she squints at him a bit, realising she left her glasses at the flat as well. She grabs her phone and sends a quick message to Jessica.

"No, and it hurts me that you think so little of me." His voice solemn and Phoebe's guilt crashes into her.

"I am sorry. I don't know what came over me."

"It's a trauma response, which I understand and I'm willing to accept, but this can't become a regular thing. Would you like me to schedule an appointment with a therapist, whether it be the one I use or I can find another one?"

"Therapy doesn't work though. I have tried it but I just hated every second of it." His shoulders relax and he moves to sit at one of the stools by the kitchen island, before nudging one over to Phoebe, a silent invitation to join him. Dean grabs two cans of monster from a bag by his feet, pulling out an original for him and an ultra-peachy keen for Phoebe. She sits down, putting her head in her hands, fighting off tears, refusing to cry when she was the one in the wrong.

"How long did you do it for?", his voice losing some of the harshness to it as he cracks open his can and takes a small sip before scrunching up his nose.

"I did it for a few months but then it got too expensive and I think maybe I thought that my trauma wasn't actually as bad as some people's." She explains, taking a massive gulp of her drink before rolling the can in her hands, finding the feeling comforting as she focuses on the movement. Roll left hand, feel texture, hold for a few seconds, roll back with right hand, repeat. Dean tracks the movement and finds it oddly soothing, tamping down on the anger bubbling under the surface, not directed at Phoebe but at the thought that she doesn't think she's worthy of getting help.

"You can't compare your trauma to someone else's or think that you are any less deserving of getting help, Squidge. I know it's a way of thinking that's hard to get out of but it's the truth."

"I know that now, but at least now I have a reason to try and get some help. Maybe I can go through the doctors to see if I can talk to someone without having to pay so much money already?" Dean hears the truth in her statement, even if she can't meet his eyes, and he gently nudges her with his knee.

"I'll get an appointment set up with the woman I see, as she's very good. Don't worry about the money side, I'll cover it." Phoebe's head snaps up and she stares at him in disbelief.

"I can't ask you to do that, I don't have the money to pay you back."

"You're not asking me to do it, I am offering and I don't want the money back. The only thing I ask is that you do this for yourself and not for anyone else."

"Isn't that a selfish thing for me to do?"

"When it comes to healing after trauma, and you've been through so much, I think it's fair for you to be selfish with healing from it, as long as you're not hurting anyone else in the process." Dean smiles softly at her and Phoebe nods weakly, before looking back down at her can, hair falling in front of her face. Dean very slowly and gently moves his hand closer to her face, pushing the hair behind her ear. He kisses her neck gently and scoots his stool closer to hers. Phoebe tenses for a second but then relaxes, before resting her head on his shoulder. He grabs his phone, and sends a message to the therapist.

Dean: Hi, do you have any hour sessions today at all? My… friend wants to start therapy, so I thought I'd see if you were free?

Cathy: Hi Dean, yes I have an opening at 5pm today, so in 2 hours. See your friend then, if you bring them that would be excellent.

Dean: Okay, thank you, see you then.

"Everything is set for you to go talk to the therapist at 5pm, so we have a few hours to kill. What would you like to do until then?" Dean says as he clicks his phone off, turning his attention to Phoebe again. A blush settles on her face and chest, her breath turning rapid and she looks at Dean from under her eyelashes.

He lets out a short breath and chuckles slightly;

"Was the attention in the aquarium not enough for you?" Phoebe whimpers slightly and Dean grabs her hand before pulling her softly to the couch in the living room.

"Are we not going to the bedroom?"

"I want to save that for if we have sex, Squidge."

"Are we not having sex now?" suspicion rising in her voice.

"I think it's still a bit too soon, trust me I want to, god I want to, but I don't want to rush this, is that okay?" She nods, relaxing a lot more. Dean notices her relax and knows that she's happy with the decision. He lies her down on the couch, before pulling up her dress so it rests on her stomach. Dean nestles in between her legs, backing up slightly before looking around and letting out a small chuckle.

"I think that we are going to need a bigger couch if this is going to become a regular occurrence." Phoebe giggles gently, like little bells flooding the space, but she quickly lets out a soft gasp as Dean hooks his fingers around the waistband of her underwear. Phoebe lifts her hips slightly and Dean pulls her underwear down her legs, chucking it somewhere in the living room. Phoebe pays it no mind as she feels his fingers inch up her thighs, tickling her skin and setting her nerves on fire. She whimpers slightly and Dean pins her with a knowing look.

"I know Squidge, let me make you feel good." His hands grip her thighs, prying her legs open. Phoebe covers her face with her hands, embarrassment flooding her body as she shivers from Deans touch.

"Don't hide from me Squidge, I want to see all of you." He reaches up and moves her hands away from her face, brushing her cheek as she nuzzles in. As she slowly opens her legs, Dean smiles against her thighs before dipping his tongue out and tracing patterns along her skin, inching towards her core. Phoebe's breath catches in her chest and Dean stops, looking up at her and arousal flushes his skin at the state of her. Eyes half shut, lips parted and panting softly. Phoebe opens her eyes all the way and looks down at him.

"Don't you dare stop unless you're uncomfortable." Dean chuckles softly and very gently runs his tongue over her folds, teasing her entrance and she lets out a groan of frustration before bucking her hips. Deans teeth run over her clit and she shudders in pleasure. He ups his efforts, swirling his tongue around her clit, dipping into her hole a little every now and then. Phoebe gets lost in the pleasure, writhing on the couch, blabbering incoherently.

"Please Dean, please I need more, anything you want." He lifts his head up, wetness soaking his chin and Phoebe lets out a gasp as she takes in the sight of him below her.

"I want you to ride my face, like you own it. I want you to take your pleasure from me."

He swiftly grabs her and changes positions so he's lying on the couch, and positions Phoebe above his face.

"Grab hold of the back, use that to steady yourself," as he speaks, Phoebe gets into position and grabs the couch so hard it creaks under her grip, "take as much as you want."

"Won't I suffocate you?"

"Then I'll die happy, now sit." His command sends a thrill of pleasure up Phoebe's spine and she slowly sits down, letting out a shaky moan as she feels the heat from his mouth on her core. His hands wrap around her thighs once more and he slowly eases her down further. His mouth covers her clit and Phoebe throws her head back in pleasure, bucking gently. She feels Dean nod from underneath her and feels his teeth scrape at her clit, sending flutters of pain and pleasure throughout her body.

"F...fuck, I didn't know this could feel so good," she begins to feel confidence brewing and she writhes on his face. Dean hardens his tongue before slowly pushing it into her tight hole, Phoebe losing all sense of control, moaning uncontrollably and thrashing like her life depends on it. She feels a tightness in her stomach and her core clenches around Dean's tongue. She shatters above him and when she looks down, he is staring right back at her, determination in his eyes. He doesn't let up his pace and swirls his tongue inside her before pulling out, taking a deep breath and then diving back in. Phoebe uses the back of the couch to help steady herself and rock on his face gently. One of Dean's hands releases its grip on her thigh, and moves underneath her. She lets out a gasp of disappointment when Dean's tongue leaves her, but its quickly replaced by a moan as he eases his finger into her, making a come hither motion with it, placing his tongue back on her clit and sending her into overdrive. Phoebe lets out a scream and Dean groans against her core when she clenches around her finger, the sounds vibrating through her. Pleasure courses through her veins and comes all over his mouth again, before collapsing slightly. Dean slowly withdraws his finger and she lets out a humph at the feeling of being so empty. Dean moves her off of his face before standing up and pulling her into his arms.

"Oh Darling, we are not quite finished yet," he says before pulling her towards the bedroom, kicking the door open and making their way to the shower.

"I know you have some trauma with showers so if you want me to stop then tell me and I will." She nods but doesn't say anything as she watches him strip out of his clothes, his muscles rippling under his skin. He sets the shower to warm and helps Phoebe stand before pushing her gently under the spray, making sure none will go in her eyes before his fingers slip between her folds again.

"I want to make you come at least once more before we get cleaned up ahead of your therapy session, is this okay?" Phoebe looks around distantly and Dean grips her chin between his finger and thumb.

"I won't do anything without your approval." She regains her senses and nods.

"I want this with you Dean; I'll tell you if it gets too much." He smiles at her before slipping one finger in her again and she gasps as the sensations flood her body once more. Her toes curl in pleasure and she lets out little moans as she feels herself teeter on the edge of climax.

"More Dean, please?" she says breathlessly.

"More, more of what Squidge?", he teases as he moves his finger in her slowly, edging her, not wanting her to creep over that line just yet. She lets out a groan of frustration and bucks her hip. Dean kisses her passionately, teeth clashing and tongues battling for dominance. Phoebe lets out a soft whimper and Dean slips in a second finger, swallowing her moans with his mouth. He rubs her walls and feels her clamp down on his fingers again, and she bites down on his shoulder as she shudders in his grasp, legs wobbling. Dean wraps his spare arm around her waist, keeping her upright as he increases the speed slightly.

"One more for me Darling, just one more." Phoebe lets out a small sob as overstimulation takes hold and she shatters quickly at his demand, feeling even more turned on at his rough voice. She feels his arousal against her thigh and she reaches down to grab his cock in her hand when he grabs her wrist.

"Don't feel pressured to do anything just because I have pleased you Squidge."

"I want to. Will you let me?" He groans in pleasure at her request before letting go of her wrist and nodding. She tentatively runs her hand over the smoothness of his skin before running her finger over the tip, smearing a mixture of pre-cum and water from the shower over it. Dean bucks into her hand and she lets out a soft giggle. This dark and brooding man, wanting her, Phoebe thinks as she slowly gets to her knees. Dean gently turns them so he is standing in the way of the water, making it hit his back rather than her face. Phoebe looks up at him and slowly opens her mouth, Dean holding his cock steady as she works her mouth around it. She gags slightly from the size and tears creep into her eyes, as she rests one of her hands on his thighs, the other coming up to grab his hand. As she runs her tongue over the vein under his cock, he lets out a throaty moan and bucks into her mouth slightly. She moans around his length and she feels him quiver in her mouth. Before he can cum in her mouth, he quickly removes himself and aims at the wall, not wanting to make Phoebe swallow something like that just yet. Phoebe smiles appreciatively and slowly rises from her knees.

"That was incredible Squidge, I had no idea your mouth would feel that good." He leans down to kiss her on the head, before opening up the body wash from the side. Scents of citrus and elderflower waft the room, making it smell undeniably like Dean. He runs his hands over her skin, massaging the body wash into a smooth lather before moving to do himself. Phoebe grabs his hand and takes the bottle, and she starts to clean him. Pride blooms in both of them as they stay stood in silence, letting it speak a thousand words as Dean proceeds to wash Phoebe's hair, slowly nudging her under the shower head to rinse her head. Phoebe holds her breath, trying to keep the panic at bay as memories flicker behind her eyelids.

"It's okay, Squidge- it's just us." She nods and opens her eyes, letting his voice ground her as they step out of the shower once they have cleaned the soap suds off of them. Dean wraps a towel around his waist and helps Phoebe out of the shower before proceeding to turn it off. A soft towel is draped across her chest and together they pad into the bedroom, both moving in tandem to sit on the bed. Dean quickly dries himself before grabbing some clean underwear and socks, pulling them on, and moving to his wardrobe. He picks out a baby blue t-shirt and some light grey shorts, dressing himself before turning to look at Phoebe, who is still perched on the end of the bed. He tilts his head and his hands fall to his sides.

"What's wrong Squidge?"

"I don't know what to wear."

"Wear whatever you feel comfortable in, it doesn't matter." He says earnestly before moving towards her clothes in one of the wardrobes. Phoebe's feet shuffle in the carpet as she stares at a spot on the floor intently.

"Would just leggings and a hoodie be okay?", she whispers.

"Yes, there's no problem with that. I know that's what you like to lounge around in." Dean grabs some leggings from one of the drawers, giving them a quick sniff and then doing the same with a baby blue hoodie. He walks back over to Phoebe, placing them beside her before turning away.

"What are you doing?" Phoebe asks curiously.

"I am giving you some privacy whilst you change Squidge." Dean fixes his eyes on a random spot on the wall, listening to her shuffle around and get dressed. He sneaks a peek and sees her back, covered in a mixture of long and short scars. He sucks in a quite breath but turns his head back, not wanting to have been caught staring.

"I'm done," she says and Dean fully turns back around, smiling at her tensely, trying not to give anything away. Phoebe walks over the hair dryer and fumbles around with the buttons for a minute before it whirs to life. She dries her hair to the point where it isn't dripping wet, before pushing it out of her face.

"Ready Squidge?" She nods in response, hands shaking slightly as she walks over to him, stopping just shy of his body. He reaches down and entwines his fingers with hers, and together they make the journey to the car.

When they reach the car, they get in and Dean heads off to the therapists, Phoebe still unaware of her name. Phoebe runs her hands over her legs anxiously, sweat slowly forming on her forehead and she lets out a shaky exhale. Her heart hammers in her chest and she looks over at Dean as he drives. His eyes flit between the road and checking the mirrors as he moves with precision and safety.

"Do you ever get bored of driving everywhere? Especially in rush hour?", she asks, his hand moving to the gear stick, dropping the car down a gear as they turn the corner.

"No, I find it relaxing most of the time. It's methodical, like there's a right way and a wrong way to do things. Yes, there are some twats on the road, but I try to not let stupid people ruin my day with their driving. Also they might be twats, but some of them might be in a hurry due to a family emergency or something like that so I try not to judge them." Phoebe ponders over his answer, watching as the high building fly by. Soon enough, they turn into an underground parking area, and Dean easily finds a spot close to the door. They swiftly get out and Dean glances at his phone, checking the time and ushering them into the elevator. The music in the elevator is soft and optimistic, helping calming the nerves that are threatening to explode out of Phoebe.

Dean runs his thumb over her hand, and with a soft ping of the elevator, they exit into the waiting area. Pretty swiftly, a woman with flowing chocolate coloured hair and piercing green eye calls Phoebes name.

"Phoebe, my name is Kathy, I'll be your therapist today, and hopefully in the future. Now unfortunately due to patient confidentiality, I am going to have to ask Dean to stay here, is that okay with you?" Phoebe looks at Dean with a brave face and he gives her a reassuring smile, picking up a trashy magazine whilst he balances his phone on his thigh.

"Go on Squidge, I'll be right here when you come out. This is a good thing." Phoebe turns to Kathy, taking in her appearance and her heart pangs in her chest.

"Have we met before? I feel like I recognise you from somewhere?"

"No I don't think so Phoebe, is something wrong?" Kathy asks politely, tilting her head whilst studying Phoebe's behaviour.

"No, sorry, you just look like someone I used to know. Ah well, they say everyone has their doppelganger." Phoebe lets out an awkward chuckle and then gives Dean a little wave as she follows Kathy down the hall, to what she assumes is her office. Phoebe can't seem to shake the feeling that she knows Kathy from somewhere, but shrugs it off for the time being.

Kathy leads them further down the brightly lit corridor, the florescent lights making Phoebe's eyes squint as she struggles to see. Someone barges into her shoulder as they hurry down the corridor, and as Phoebe turns to apologise, the person is long gone. When she turns back around, Kathy is waiting with a perfectly manicured hand holding a dark brown wooden door open. Tentatively, Phoebe pokes her head round the corner, seeing a few different coloured and textured chairs dotted around, an assortment of fidget toys in a box and a green fluffy carpet pushed to one side of the room. Phoebe takes a step in and allows herself to calm down slightly before moving out of the doorway, letting Kathy come in and take the lead. Kathy takes a seat in a chair with a little desk attached to it, before leaning down and taking off her shoes, burying her feet in the softness of the rug, letting out a sigh of happiness.

"Come in and make yourself comfortable Phoebe, you can sit anywhere you like and there are things you can fiddle with if you want. I know the 'first' therapy session can be quite daunting." Phoebe shuffled over to a beige cuddle sofa in the corner of the room, grabbing a stuffed starfish from the side and holding it close to her chest. The light yellow walls seemingly warm her skin and calm her anxieties down a bit, and Phoebe takes the time to really look at Kathy. Eyebrows drawn on, plum lips, high cheekbones, long legs crossed over each other, a black dress that falls to just above her knees. Still, Phoebe couldn't shake the feeling that she had met Kathy somewhere.

"I know you think you have seen me from somewhere or know me, but I can assure you I wouldn't take on anyone that I know personally as that's highly unprofessional. Now shall we talk about why you are here?" Kathy looks at her attentively, but Phoebe can't meet her eyes. Phoebe takes a deep breath, releasing it slowly before starting to speak.

"I'm here because I need help, I'm not sure what I'm going to get out of this but I really want to start my healing journey and learn how to manage my PTSD attacks and triggers."

"That's a good starting point and definitely something we can work with Phoebe, so let's go to the memory that has the most 'power' over you in some ways. Can you walk me through what happened?" Phoebe closes her eyes, eyelids flickering as her memories threaten to overwhelm her as she sifts through her trauma, trying to pinpoint the right one.

"It wasn't the first time I was hurt physically, but I think this is the one that holds the most trauma as such..." Phoebe looks at Kathy who nods at her in understanding before continuing; "I had started dating this boy in my first year of university, and within a few weeks I knew that it wasn't going well, but I was dealing with the loss of my grandad and I had moved five hours away from my parents, so I needed someone." Phoebe looks down at the cuddly starfish, its eyes looking up at her, and hope tingles underneath her skin at the idea of Kathy not turning her away and saying her trauma is 'too much to deal with'.

"He lived three hours away, so when he would stay over, he'd stay for up to a week with me. The first time we met, it was magical and we couldn't keep our hands off of each other. But that quickly changed, he was into some... unusual kinks... and because I was relatively new to sex, I wasn't sure what I was into, but I was willing to try everything once to see if I would enjoy it.

One day, he asked if I would be into doing stuff in the shower, but I really don't like water in my face, but he dragged me by my hair into the shower, shoving my head under the shower and holding it there... as he... " Phoebe took a shaky breath, chest tightening and she mutters, "he... raped me... whilst kind of drowning me. I couldn't breathe, everything hurt and I felt like my body was going to snap in half." Tears stream down Phoebe's face as she looks up at Kathy, sympathy etched on her face. Phoebe lets out a choked gasp, feeling like her world is falling apart.

"Did you try talking to your parents about this?", her face furrowing in confusion.

"They were dealing with the loss of my grandad at the time as well, I didn't want them to have to deal with this as well. I thought that I would be able to end the relationship and save myself." Phoebe shuffles in the seat, suddenly very uncomfortable as Kathy begins to write in her little notebook on the desk. As she places the pen down, she gestures at Phoebe to continue.

"That wasn't even the worst part..." Phoebe looks up to the ceiling, praying none of this will come back to bite her on the ass. "The next time he stayed over, because I was so stupid to let him back, he apologised profusely and swore he would never hurt me again. But it was all lies, that I should have seen. One night we had been drinking, and I said I was interested in being tied up, not a lot, just my hands or something but he took it too far. I had a desk that went along one wall and then slightly down another, and it had thick metal legs that were drilled into the floor. So whilst I was slightly tipsy, he pulled me under the desk and wrapped my hands to those metal legs with duct tape. It was so uncomfortable, and he left me like that for days. He refused to untie me to let me eat or use the toilet, so he would force feed me and would hold a bowl underneath me so I could pee. He used me in so many ways, and my flatmates had no idea, because I used to sleep through the day, he would just say I was asleep whenever they asked where I was." Phoebe lets out a chokes gasp and starts crying uncontrollably, Kathy sitting there, patiently waiting for Phoebe to get it out of her system. Phoebe gets herself together and buries her face in the starfish again, embarrassed that she didn't end the relationship sooner.

"When did you decide enough was enough?", Kathy taps the pen rhythmically, the sound grounding Phoebe and allowing her to focus on the session, even as she feels an attack brewing in her chest.

"When I was talking to my friends, and they said that what was happening wasn't normal. They didn't know all the details but I think they figured some bits out." Phoebe moves to lie on the rug, staring up at the ceiling, looking at the swirling patterns.

"Who do you hold responsible for the trauma?"

"Myself…"

"Why?"

"Because I moved away, even though I needed to, and I latched on to the first person who showed me the slightest bit of affection. I had just lost one of the most important people in my life, I hated being back home, AND I NEEDED AN OUT!!!" She screamed the last part, anger flooding her veins and her face turning red. Hands gripped at her hair, pulling slightly but not hard enough to cause too much damage. Kathy doesn't flinch at her outburst, but speaks gently.

"Why do you not blame the man who hurt you?"

"I don't know, maybe because it's not his fault, maybe he had a bad upbringing or something and that was his version of love, but it didn't work for me?" Phoebe whispers, letting out little hiccups as she tries to calm down enough to continue the session.

"No person is meant to hurt another person, no matter how messed up their childhood is. It doesn't give them a right to hurt you, but unfortunately some people's brains are wired a bit different to ours."

"How do I move on from this? How do I get over this trauma?" Phoebe says pleadingly.

"I don't think there is a way to 'get over trauma' but there are definitely ways to manage the triggers and come to terms with what happened." Kathy speaks patiently, making sure that Phoebe understands what she is saying. Phoebe ponders that statement for a few minutes before letting out another shaky exhale.

"I honestly don't know if I'll ever be able to come to terms with what happened, and I don't know what my triggers are until they happen. Like earlier... someone... put their phone on the table, screen face down and I lost my shit at them, thinking they were hiding something or someone from me, when all they have done is shown me nothing but patience, love and respect. What's wrong with me to act like that?"

"When was the last time you relaxed and did something for yourself? From what I've gathered, you have gone straight into working after university and you're still processing everything that happened to you a few years ago. You've essentially been stuck in fight or flight this whole time," Ouch, Phoebe thought, and that must have shown on her face, as Kathy continues, "I didn't mean that in any disrespect but maybe you need to go on a small holiday somewhere or do something you have always wanted to do." Phoebe nods slightly, knowing that she won't be going on a holiday, especially if Joel is still around. No where is safe.

"For our next session, I'd like for you to have figured out a few of your triggers and made a list of them to bring with you. Don't go out of your way to find those triggers, but if they do arise then just make a little note of them and how they made you feel in that moment."

"I can do that, I think. I can maybe get Dean to help me..." Kathy pins her with a disapproving look.

"No, I think it's best if you try and do this for yourself, as Dean might not write the correct phrases or how you were feeling right. This needs to be you, as this is your healing journey." Phoebe nods sheepishly, a bit embarrassed at being reprimanded by someone of similar age, and she pushes herself off of her back and onto her feet.

"Thank you for seeing me, can we schedule another appointment?"

"Does next Thursday work for you?", Kathy says as she flicks through a planner, making sure that she is free that day.

"Yes, I can do anytime."

"Fabulous, let's arrange for 11am, and I look forward to seeing you next week." She stays seated as Phoebe moves for the door. She casts one last look at Kathy before opening the door and heading down the hall, back to Dean.

When she sees him leaning against a wall, she runs into his arms, jumping up and wrapping her legs around him. He lets out an oof as she slams into him, but quickly picks her up, hands resting on her backside as he feels her nuzzle into his neck.

"I am so proud of you for taking this first step Squidge," he murmurs, kissing the top of her head and sniffing her hair slightly. She murmurs something back but he can't quite make out the words, her voice muffled by his top and crook of his neck. Dean carries her out the reception and down to the car, ignoring the judgemental glances he gets from people.

"God, can't she walk herself, does she have to be carried around like a baby?" an elderly lady sneers, turning her nose up at the sight. Dean turns around slowly, glaring at the old bat who quickly (well as quickly as an old lady can) shuffles away from them.

"Yeah, that's what I thought", he mutters before somehow managing to unlock his car with one hand, opening the passenger door, and carefully placing Phoebe on the seat. He quickly runs around to his side, jumps in the seat and reverses out of the parking spot. Phoebe stares out the window, lost in her own head, a mixture of happy and traumatising memories battling together, each one threatening to overturn the other.

"Would you like to talk about how it went?" She shakes her head.

"No, I don't think I'm ready to share what myself and Kathy spoke about just yet. But we did agree that I would make a list of triggers and how they affected me, ahead of our session next Thursday." She glances over to him, scared of his reaction, but he just nods thoughtfully.

"Yeah, that sounds about right. Also just letting you know now, your boss has been calling you nonstop today, it's been driving me insane, so when we get home, I've got to make a couple of work calls, so could you give him a ring back please?"

"Yes, of course, I wonder what he wants since there's been no work for me the past few weeks, so hopefully there is some."

"Yeah I wonder", he says nonchalantly. Phoebe pays his tone no mind, knowing he always gets into his own head when work is involved. They sit together in silence as they pull into the apartment parking complex and they walk up the stairs to Dean's apartment.

Dean instantly steps into the bedroom to make a few calls, his voice already rising slightly. Phoebe knows his line of work is stressful, so she tries to tamp down on the anxiety moving under her skin. She grabs her phone from the pocket of her hoodie, finger hovering over the contact button for Benny, hesitating slightly at what he could want. Phoebe jumps out of her skin at the phone going off in her hand, and she answers when she sees its Benny.

"Hi Benny, how are you?"

"Yeah hi Phoebe, look it's going to be a quick one since we are so busy here right now, but unfortunately I am going to have to let you go."

"What why?"

"Well it's come to my attention that you have accused a friend of mine of rape, and I can't tolerate that in my store, so whilst this has made my life a bit hectic, I think it's for the best and I never want to see you here again, even as a customer." Before Phoebe can form a rebuttal, the line disconnects and she stares at the phone in shock. Dean comes out of the bedroom looking frazzled, running his hands through his hair and letting out a groan of frustration.

"I am guessing your phone call didn't go well either then?" she says shyly, not wanting to set him off. He shakes his head and his hands quake in anger, and he lashes out at the wall, slamming his fist through the dry wall before taking it out and shaking off the pain. His face glances up to Phoebe and turns pale at the sight of her distressed state.

"You fucking whore Phoebe, why would you look at that man like that?!" Joel screams in her face, her turning away from him but he grabs her hair, pulling it back tight forcing her to look at him. She whimpers in pain, hands reaching up to try and yank his hands off.

"I'm so sorry Squidge, I wasn't thinking, please... I would never lay a hand on you, ever." Phoebes stomach clenches and rolls as the flashbacks overwhelm her senses and the line between past and present gets blurry.

Joel slaps her hands away from his hand, before grabbing her wrists and squeezing them so tightly, Phoebe thinks her bones are going to break.

"Maybe it's time to teach you a lesson, you little ungrateful bitch." He uses her hair to guide her to her knees, the carpet scraping against her skin and tears stream down her face. He keeps his grip on her wrists and quickly lets go of her hair, grabbing a piece of rope of the table.

"N... no, please, not again, I promise I'll be good..." she cries, trying to wriggle away from the rope, fear taking over her body. Joel smiles maliciously, and makes quick work of tying her hands together before looping the bit of rope over a hook hanging from the bedroom ceiling. He pulls it tight, Phoebe's arms pulled above her head and she lets out a howl of pain as her shoulders pop out of place.

"Now be a good little puppet and don't move, I need to tie this off so you can't get away from me." He keeps the rope pulled tight, not allowing any slack, as he then ties the rope around Phoebe's thigh, looping it once, twice, thrice before linking it to the other one and repeating the process. He uses the last of the rope to loop it back over the hook in the ceiling, yanking it as hard can go, so that Phoebe is suspend on her tummy in mid-air with her wrists and thighs pointing towards the ceiling. She screams in pain as she feels her shoulders pop out of their sockets and her legs stretch and Joel lets out an evil cackle as he paces around her, stripping off his clothes.

"Aren't you looking good, all trussed up for me like a little piggie." He runs his finger over her back, watching as she quivers in fear before he stands in front of her. He grabs her hair and pulls tight, eliciting a scream from her, it piercing the air and Joel lets out a groan of pleasure.

"Fuck me Phoebe, I can't wait to be in you again, although I will say, it's not nearly as fun as pinning you down. But since you like looking at men so much, I thought this would be a great learning opportunity for you." He produces a metal gag with a hole in the middle, and as Phoebe clamps her mouth shut, he pinches her nose forcing it open and the gag in. She twists her head but Joel is quick with securing the buckle in place, pulling it so tight she feels like her head is going to explode. Joel whistles and as two tall men walk in, Phoebes gaze turns to the floor, recognising one of them as Pitch- a vile man who gives Joel a run for his money.

"Don't be shy, Phoebe—you were eager to look before." He grabs her face, tilting it to meet all three of theirs, them grinning menacingly down at her. Joel walks around and rips her underwear away from her body, slamming into her in one thrust. Phoebe lets out a muffled scream from behind the gag and the men groan in pleasure.

"Phoebe, I promise I won't let Joel hurt you ever again, but I need you to stop screaming, please Darling."

"Keep screaming Phoebe, it only gets us off more." Joel jerks his head and the two men move over to where Phoebe is hanging, touching and groping her. Pitch's finger prods at her puckered entrance as the other man's finger runs along the metal piece of

the gag. They both dip into the respective holes simultaneously and Phoebe groans out in pain, thrashing as much as she can in her bonds. One of the men thrusts into her mouth, causing her to gag and scream in discomfort. Pitch thrusts his finger into her ass and she fights as much as she can. The cock in her mouth presses against the back of her throat and she struggles to breath. A hand pinches her nose and she falls out of consciousness...

"Phoebe? Can you hear me?" She whimpers in response and throws herself into Dean's open arms.

"Make me forget, please. Replace the bad memories with ones with you."

"I'm not sure that is a good idea Darling, you've just relived something traumatic." She lets out a soft sob and tears dampen his shirt.

"Please Dean, I need this, I want to chase the memories away and make new, better ones." He lets out a sigh and nods against her head.

Chapter Ten

"**I** need you to promise if it gets too much, you tell me to stop and no matter what I will, okay Squidge?"

"I promise Dean, please make the pain go away." He holds her tight for a few minutes, muttering sweet nothings in her ear and she smiles against his chest. He lifts her gently from the floor, and he carries her over to the bedroom, softly placing her on the bed, before turning on the red led light in the corner. He turns around to lock the door and when he turns back, Phoebe has stripped off her clothes, leaving her bare for him to see. She turns her back to him, allowing him to see her scars for the first time of her own volition. He takes a sharp breath and slowly runs his fingers along the scars. Phoebe lets out a gasp.

"Can you feel me when I touch you there?"

"In some places yes, but it's mostly numb from nerve damage." Dean's eyes flash with anger at the amount of trauma Phoebe has been through, but doesn't say anything more, his hands sliding down over her hips and he pulls her flush against him. She lets out a throaty moan as she feels his length grind into her and she tests a bit by wiggling back into him. He laughs softly, nipping at her ear before moving to kiss down her neck. Phoebe turns quickly in his grasp and pulls at his shirt and shorts.

"Off, please."

"So polite Squidge." He accepts her cute demand and pulls the shirt over his head, loving the fact that Phoebe takes her time running her eyes along his chest and arms. He flexes slightly and she giggles before tapping her foot and looking at his shorts expectantly. Dean quickly pulls his shorts and boxers down, tossing them to the growing pile of clothes. They move in one motion to the bed, Dean hovering over Phoebe as she lays on her back against the soft sheets and pillows to keep her propped up. He slowly works his way down to her core, blowing on it gently, Phoebe grips his hair and pushes him closer.

"Such a greedy little thing aren't you Squidge", he murmurs and goes to lick at her folds, but quickly turns his head and kisses the insides of her thighs.

"Dean please, don't tease me, I want this... oh god..." He runs his tongue along her folds, staring up at her as her eyes roll back in pleasure. The tip of his tongue dips into her hole and her hands fist the sheets, writhing on the bed slowly, grinding up into his mouth. Dean laps and slurps, obscene noises flooding the bedroom as Phoebe moans uncontrollably. Pink rises on her cheeks and her legs shake as Dean wraps his hands around them, pulling her closer to him. He lets out a moan of pleasure and feasts down on her as if she is his last meal. Her pussy clamps down and she gushes into his mouth with a scream. Dean pulls back looking very proud of himself as he slowly work his way up her body. His hands find her tits, gently palming them before running a finger over her nipples. Phoebe shivers in ecstasy and Dean drops his head, swirling his tongue around one whilst rolling the other between his fingers. Her legs wrap around his waist and pull him closer as she holds onto his hair for dear life. Phoebe rocks her pussy against his dick, feeling it growing even more, she reaches down to stroke it but Dean pins her hands above her head, shaking his head still with her nipple in his mouth.

"Dean please, I want to cum over your cock, please let me." He releases her nipple with a pop.

"You beg so sweetly Darling, how am I meant to stay no to you? Let me show you what a real man can do to this amazing body. Let me worship you." He lets go of her other nipple, grabs the base of his cock and gently runs the tip over her folds, making her moan again.

"I definitely think I have found my new favourite sound, that and those little whimpers you do when we are trying to be discreet." She thrashes on the bed and Dean presses the tip of his cock inside, watching as her mouth forms a small 'o'. He dips his head again and kisses her like his life depends on it. Teeth clash, tongues battle for dominance, and moans are swallowed. Dean presses a little more inside her, groaning at her welcoming heat embracing him. He feels the walls of her pussy flutter around him and he breaks from the kiss, touching her forehead with his own. Phoebes eyes flutter open and Dean looks at her for any hesitation, finding none he pushes further in, keeping his eyes on her. Phoebe pants as she feels him fill her up, inch by delectable inch, making her toes curl. With one final thrust, Dean works himself all the way in and stays still, waiting for Phoebe to adjust to his size. He didn't want to risk hurting her or triggering something, so he leans down and nuzzles into her neck, letting himself feel her around him, knowing he could die a happy man. Though if he did die, Phoebe would find a way to bring him back to life. Phoebe whimpers from below him and he feels her pussy relax around him. When he feels her hips buck slightly, he lifts his head, and seeing the impatience on her face, he starts to thrust very slowly, groaning as he holds himself back. Dean threads his fingers through hers and rest his forehead on hers again, keeping eye contact as she watches his face contort to one of pleasure. She nods against him and his thrusts gets quicker, her own hips rising to meet his. Phoebe keeps her legs wrapped around him, using the leverage to drag him back in any time he moves out.

"Someone's enjoying themselves," he whispers, watching as she nods rapidly. His cock grows harder inside her, so he uses one of his hands to move down her body, towards her clit. His finger finds the magic button quickly and sets a relenting pace as he leans down and sucks on her nipple again. Phoebe squirms in his hold, overstimulation creeping up her toes and legs.

"Dean, please, I'm going to cum, can you come with me?" she shivers, bucking her hips like a wild animal. He groans against her nipple, sending white hot pleasure racing down her spine and she clenches around him. With one final flourish, Phoebe screams and cums all over his dick, Dean quickly following suit and unloading into her. He stays inside her, thrusting slowly as his dick slowly calms down and then he withdraws, Phoebe whimpering at the sudden loss and emptiness. Dean huffs out a laugh.

"Still hungry for more Darling?" she nods, "well how about we give something else a try because I'm knackered but I want to keep pleasing you." She nods again and shivers as he traces the outline of her nipples. He reaches into a drawer and pulls out a dildo. Phoebe eyes it slowly, still trying to catch her breath when she notices something.

"Yep, I stuck my dick in a mould for you, Darling." Phoebe bursts out laughing and Dean chuckles along with her. He grabs the base and runs the tip against her folds again before working into her. Dean feels her clench around the mould and he starts thrusting it in and out of her, watching intently as she trembles and whimpers in his bed. He kisses along her scars before making his way up to her neck, whispering praise in her ear.

"You're so beautiful like this Squidge, I want to see you come apart like this every day if you'll let me." She moans in response, happy to agree to anything if it gets her feeling like this again. She shatters over the dildo and moves her hands down to push it out of her.

"No more, please." Dean eases it out of her, not wanting to yank it out, before chucking it towards the bathroom, so it reminds him to clean it properly later. He wraps his arms around her and pulls her on top of his chest.

"Was that okay? I didn't go too hard did I?" she shakes her head against his chest, feeling to euphoric to try and get any more words out. He kisses the top of her head, before they both drift off to sleep for a while.

When they both arise, they are tangled up in each other's limbs, sweat and bodily fluids clinging to them. Dean and Phoebe both yawn slightly, looking over at the clock on the bedside table. 8pm. Shit. Dean looks over at Phoebe and her stomach lets out an almighty roar, causing her to squeak in embarrassment, hiding her face in his chest.

"Alright, lets order some food Squidge, I don't want to have to deal with a hangry you, I've heard enough of the horror stories from Jessica, thank you very much." Pheobe cackles at that, knowing it's true, both of them quickly ordering from Dominoes before starting to clean up the bedroom and throwing on some pyjamas. They move to the living room and Dean pours a glass of wine from them each before he sits in his chair and Phoebe sits in her designated spot. They both take a sip of the wine, and sighing deeply. A few moments pass, and just as Dean goes to flick the television on, Phoebe blurts out.

"Dean, I am worried that my anxiety isn't going to get better no matter how much work I do, and that I am going to keep having panic attacks." She looks down in shame. Dean rises to his feet and then crouches in front of her, tilting her head up to meet his gaze.

"As long as you're trying, that is the main thing Squidge. No one will be able to keep me away from you. We all have our traumas but that doesn't define us."

"But what if it doesn't get better?" she whispers. He bumps his nose against hers,

"It will. It'll take time, patience and even a bit of anger, but it will get better, that much I can promise you. Any time you fall down, either myself, Jessica or Kathy will be right there to pick you up, okay?" She nods against him and they snuggle onto the sofa together, watching crappy tv until their food arrives. They stuff their faces with carbs and meat until they pass out together tucked in each other's arms on the sofa, where they stay until morning.

Chapter Eleven

Over the next few months, Dean and Phoebe fall into what would be described as a somewhat normal life. Dean worked from home most of the time, answering multiple calls a day and Phoebe sees Kathy twice a week. Together the two of them have created an unstoppable machine as Phoebe helps Dean with his business as and where she can. Dean still looks for Joel, but all seems quiet on that front, but Phoebe knows better than to think he is gone for good. She paces back and forth in the flat, restless.

"We are going to find him Squidge, but maybe he has moved on to his next target", Phoebe glares at him and he visibly gulps, "never mind, ignore me. I've got a team of people working in shifts trying to find this guy, and when we do, we will be ready." Phoebe rolls her shoulders, the ache from their earlier work out being a pleasant distractions from the thoughts swirling inside her head. She counts backwards from ten, grounding herself, focusing on the present. Dean stares at her, unmoving and not speaking, letting her do her thing. Pride washes over him at how far she has come in the past few months. There's still things she needs to work on, like communicating better rather than shutting down, but Dean is patient, knowing that she isn't giving him the silent treatment anymore.

"I just know he's out there, plotting some kind of revenge. Plus he's good with cameras and security, I don't think we will find him unless he wants us too." Dean listens intently and nods, taking on board what she is saying.

"I understand, not fully but I get the feeling of the unknown can be overwhelming. But on the flip side, him backing off or biding his time has allowed you to get stronger and not just physically. You haven't had a PTSD attack in a week and you managed to defend yourself against Jack, so that's something." Phoebe nods absentmindedly, tapping her fingers on her thighs before turning to look at Dean.

"Can I have Jessica come over whilst you are at your therapists? I haven't seen her in a while and it would be nice to catch up."

"Yes of course, she's on the approved guest list so it'll be no trouble for her to get through reception and security." Over the past month, Dean and Phoebe had upped the security to the maximum, explaining to the residents what was going on, and thankfully they all understood. Dean grabs his jacket from the island and shrugs it over his shoulders. Phoebe whips out her phone and sends a quick text to Jessica.

Phoebe: Hey Jess! Sorry I haven't messaged much lately; would you like to come over for girls night?

She receives a text back instantly, quickly looking as Dean pops his shoes on.

Jessica: Hey girl! Would love to. I'll be there in ten, just gonna grab some wine and snacks. Do I need a code or anything to get in?

Phoebe: Nope, you're on the approved welcome list, just show them your ID when you get here, and if you have any problems then let me know and I'll come down.

Jessica: Sounds good! See you soon.

She pops her phone back on the coffee table, standing up as Dean walks to the door.

"All good with Jessica?"

"Yeh she's on her way, just going to stop at the store on the way here," he goes to open the door, "oh one more thing." She races into his arms and tackles him in a hug, before kissing him deeply, running her hands through his hair. He moans softly, groaning as he pulls away, looking at his watch.

"We'll continue this when I'm back. But have fun Squidge, and I'll see you later." He gives her a peck on the cheek and walks out the door. As soon as he leaves, Phoebe locks all the latches on the door and pulls up the security feed on her tablet, setting it on the side as she cleans up the mess that her and Dean made from lunch. She pops utensils and pans in the dishwasher and starts sweeping the floor, making sure to get all the crumbs out of the corners. Time flies by and before she realises it, two hours have gone past. Phoebe looks around at the now spotless flat before noticing the time.

"What... the... fuck...?" She grabs her phone in a panic and calls Jessica, the phone going straight to voicemail. Her heart surges and she pushes the panic button to unlock their emergency panic room. Her hands shake as she dials again, hoping that Jessica's phone had just died. No response again. Phoebe calls Dean, wondering if he's heard from Jessica and maybe he's helping her out with something. No response.

"Oh fucking bollocks!" She explodes. She reaches for her gun, taser and knife, hiding them in the waistband of her leggings before pulling on her trainers. She has no idea where they could be, but she decides to start at Kathy's and then make her way to the supermarket that Jessica always uses. Before she can make a move, her phone pings with a message. She opens it but drops her phone in horror. There on the screen, was a picture of Jessica and Dean beaten and bloody, tied to two chairs facing each other. Phoebe throws herself over the sink and empties the content of her stomach, before wiping her mouth and gargling some water. Her phone lets out an eerie ring, piercing the silence. No caller ID. She picks up.

"Hello?"

"Well well well, what a predicament your little friends seem to have gotten themselves into by knowing you." Joel's creepy voice wafts down the phone and Phoebe nearly drops it again. Guilt crashes into her.

"Oh poor baby, has the bad man got the people you care about?"

"What do you want Joel?", she spits out his name like it's poison in her mouth.

"Oh Darling" her stomach flips at his use of one of Dean's pet names for her, "isn't it obvious. I want you back here with me, we used to have so much fun together. Don't you remember? We have so many good memories, we even tried to start a family together before you became a murderer."

"What the fuck are you talking about Joel? I am not a murderer, although I'll probably kill you for hurting the people I love."

"Well you see, when you tried to kill yourself all those years ago, I never did get a thank you for saving you by the way, you didn't know this, but you were pregnant." The silence was so loud it was deafening. Phoebe's blood rushed from her face and she turns to look at the mirror.

"I was pregnant?" she whispers down the phone. He hums in response.

"Now, how far would you be willing to go for your 'found family', are you going to be able to save them, unlike your own flesh and blood. Mummy and daddy put up one hell of a fight, I'll give them that, but in the end they met their sticky fate for trying to keep us apart."

"What do you want me to do?"

"I want us to be a family again, I'm sure we can keep Jessica, she's been so accommodating already with myself and Pitch, I think we shall keep her." His voice comes through the phone like slime, and Phoebe gags as it washes over her. Rage pounds through her blood and her fist clenches by her side.

"Don't fucking touch her. Tell me where you are, I'll come to you, and you can have me, I'll never try to run away or escape again. You can have your perfect doll again, but they need to be released." A beat of silence passes between them before Joel lets out a sigh.

"Fine, I'm sure I can talk to Pitch to get him to agree. I'll send you the coordinates but come alone. If I get a single sense that you brought backup, I'll put a bullet in-between their eyes like I did with dear old mum and dad." Phoebe clenches her teeth, and stares down at the phone so intently, before Joel hangs up on her. She lets out a scream before opening the door and running out into the hallway, finding Jack leaning against the wall. She pulls him round the corner and Jack looks at her terror-stricken face, a pit forming in the bottom of his stomach.

"Pheebs? What's wrong? You've never touched me before unless it's for training."

"Joel. He's got Dean and Jessica."

"Well that's not good, what's the plan?" He asks, already messaging Piper and Leon as he listens to Phoebe.

"Come to this warehouse, I'll send you the coordinates, I don't trust him to not to have somehow tapped my phone to see if I call anyone." Jack quickly takes a picture.

"Me taking a picture is better, he might be able to see if you send texts as well. How are we going to play this? I am going to assume he told you not to bring anyone."

"Correct but I am not that thick. I want you to bring yourself, obviously, Piper and Leon. You three are the stealthiest and that's what we need right now. I am going to pretend I'm alone but I need you to find a weak spot, maybe see if you can borrow any of Archies gear to help you." Jack nods, his blonde hair bobbing slightly, not wanting to argue with Phoebe on this one.

"You need to tell him Phoebe. Don't wait any longer, it's so obvious."

She nods and runs down the hallway, heading straight to Dean's car. She has no idea what it's called, only that Dean uses it in emergencies because it's so fast. Phoebe looks at the dash, noticing ten minutes have already gone by, so she quickly shoots out of the parking lot, ignoring the constant beeping of the car telling her to put her seat belt on. She flips it off as she turns a corner, slightly mounting the kerb before straightening out again. She follows the GPS to the warehouse and double checks she still has her gun, taser and knife in her waistband. Phoebe opens the door, and slowly makes her way to the entrance, the dark building seeming to have another worldly glow to it. Her eyes scanned the windows looking for any sign of movement, before she notices a light switch on. She focuses on the window as she drops down to a crouch and slowly moves that way, startling as flood lights turn on, illuminating the area. A crackle comes through the speakers.

"Come on Phoebe, you really think that you can sneak up on me like that?" A laugh sounded through, like nails on a chalk board. Phoebe rolls her eyes at his theatrics, standing up right and walking straight through the front door. She pulls out her knife, gripping her grip firm as she hides it behind her wrist, trying to keep it out of sight until needed. She rounds a corner and fear takes hold as she sees what's in front of her. Baby shoes hanging from the ceiling, photos of her and Dean, photos of her Grandad, photos of her at her old job. He'd been watching her for so long, and she had no idea. Vomit threatens to crawl its way up her throat but she swallows and pushes it down. She needs to save her family.

A door was ajar to the left and she pushes it open quickly with her foot. There in the middle of the room, were her two favourite people, tied up and in pain. Joel stood with his back to her, a knife in one hand and a whip in the other, his two favourite torture devices. He didn't turn fully but he glances over his shoulder, tilting his head slightly.

"Phoebe, welcome home Darling." Phoebe stops trying to creep up on him and turned to look at the room. Whilst the rest of the building was in disarray, Joel had managed to somehow change this room to look exactly like their old room. Phoebe gulps and stands as still as a statue. Dean groans and lifts his head, eyes blazing in fury and fear as he looks at Joel and Phoebe respectively. Phoebe never thought she would truly be back in this man's clutches, and fear threatens to overwhelm her. Joel turns to her, a sick twisted smile etched across his face and he walks behind her, draping his arm over her shoulder and digging the knife into her side.

"Chuck all your weapons over in that corner," he gestures vaguely with his knife, keeping an eye on his two captives, "I know you have them on you." She tosses them, a whimper creeping from her throat. She goes to kick Joel in the nuts but a tut sounds from behind them. Phoebe turns her head to see long legs crossed over each other, sitting on a chair in the corner of the room. Dark brown hair falls over strong shoulders, and the woman's legs uncross, a black dress falling just above the knee.

"Kathy?" Phoebe asks in disbelief, shaking her head as she watches the woman rise from the chair and stalking over to her. She slaps Phoebe across the face, causing her to gasp out in pain, her head whipping to the side; Dean and Jessica scream profanities at Kathy.

"You fucking bitch, all this time, you were working with this dickhead?! I opened up to you, I trusted you, and this is what happens!" She screams, twisting in Joel's hold, not caring that the knife is digging into her skin, blood trickling down and bleeding through her top. He struggles to hold her but regains his grip and anchors himself better.

"I'm honestly so surprised you didn't figure it out. You were so sure that you had seen me before, but clearly you are as thick as you look because you never put two and two together." Kathy tilts her head, studying her like she has done for the past few months, before letting out a maniacal cackle.

"I knew I wasn't crazy."

"No you weren't, you want to know? Well, I'll tell you anyways. I was at the charity foundation thing that Joel was hosting, and I was the one that told him you were looking at other men. As if you needed anyone else but Joel. He cared about you, he wanted to marry you and you had the audacity to go whoring around and eyeing up other men." Silence floods the room, to the point you could hear a pin drop. Phoebe remains extremely calm as she speaks.

"So you're the reason I was raped by multiple men at once."

"Yep! Now you're getting it," Kathy says gleefully, "all I had to do was plant some seeds here, throw a few curveballs there, and it all came together." Phoebe's fury rushes to the surface and she kicks Joel's bad knee, remembering which one it was and launches herself at Kathy. She lets out a shriek of surprise, giving Phoebe the opening she needed. Hours of training with Jack, Dean, Piper and Leon had taught her to use her quickness to her advantage. Phoebe straddled Kathy and begins to repeatedly punch Kathy in the face, blood spraying from the force of her hits.

"ENOUGH!!!" Joel screams, and Phoebe turns her head to look at him. His eyes wild and holding two guns, one at her best friends head, and one at Dean's. She halts her raised fist and rises slowly.

"Joel don't do this, please."

"Swear you'll come with us and you won't leave me again," his voice begging, almost pleading. She drops to her knees in front of the chairs, looking up at two of the most important people in her life. They shake their heads, but Joel bashes their heads with the butt of the guns, causing them to groan in pain. Dean tries to work his way out of the ropes binding him and Jessica stares at Phoebe, pleading for her not to do this.

"I swear, but please, just let them live. I won't run away; I won't try and contact them." He smiles victoriously.

"That's my girl", he says, crouching down in front of her as she feels her wrists being pulled behind her. His lips meet hers and

Phoebe clenches her stomach, trying not to throw up. A smash of glass sounded around them and Joel instantly jumps to his feet, before letting out an oomph and a scream as he is shot in the arm. Phoebe grins and looks at her best friend and Dean who stare at her in confusion. The calvary had arrived.

Chapter Twelve

Gunshots ring out across the warehouse, Phoebe ducking as Joel screams in frustration.

"PHOEBE YOU LITTLE BITCH! I TOLD YOU TO COME ALONE!!!" Phoebe laughs humorously, as Dean and Jessica struggle in their bonds.

"You think I'd ever listen to you after everything you have done to me?" Phoebe takes aim and fires at Joel, and he lets out a shriek as the bullet goes wide and fires into the wall by his head. Joel runs out the door and Phoebe goes to follow, but a grunt of pain stops her in her tracks. She slowly turns and sees Dean yanking his arms as hard as he can. Phoebe gulps, knowing for experience that those knots will hold until someone releases you. She runs over and starts to untie him but stops when she takes in the sight of his back. Angry red welts litter his skin, thin lines of blood trickle down and his shirt is torn to pieces. Tears flood her eyes but her fingers make swift work of the ropes, tugging his free. Dean struggles to his feet, fighting off the nausea swirling in his stomach, his bare feet trembling on the floor and he attempts to steady himself.

"Be careful Dean, you're hurt."

"I knew you'd come for us, it's okay Squidge, it looks worse than it is." He says playfully, nudging her with his shoulder before groaning at the movement. Phoebe grabs his arm and holds him up, quickly looking at Jessica.

"I really shouldn't have gone to the shops," she grins lopsidedly as she lets out a soft huff of pain. Her hair is all over her face, bruises littering her face, and her shoulder stuck at an awkward angle.

"The fucker popped my shoulder, be a dear and untie me so I can pop it back in?" Phoebe stares at her in shock before quickly untying her, glancing at the door every second as more gunshots ring out across the warehouse. Phoebe takes a sharp intake, knowing Joel is a slippery weasel, and he often doesn't work alone.

"Okay all done, Dean can you pop it back in?"

"I can try Darling." He stands behind Jessica, grabbing her shoulder and her arm, then yanking it back. Jessica lets out a scream, causing Phoebe to slam her hand over Jessica's mouth. Jessica lets out a muffled 'kinky' and licks Phoebe's hand. Phoebe giggles and looks over at Dean as he does a one over of Jessicas shoulder.

"That should start feeling better but we should probably get that checked out when we get out of here."

"If we get out of here," Phoebe mutters. They both stare at her as if she'd kicked their dog, "what? The odds aren't completely in our favour. You two are hurt, Joel and Kathy are on the run and we have no idea where they could be, and we have no clue how many people Joel has hidden around, because he never works alone, trust me."

"We need to move. If we are going to catch every fucker in here, then we need to start moving." Dean rolls his shoulders, wincing in pain before scouring the place, looking for any spare weapons they can use. Phoebe's eyes light up as she stares at the room that haunted her for years. She quickly moves over to a floorboard before grabbing a screwdriver on the floor, using it to lift it up. Underneath the floorboard was two knives and a few guns.

"Bingo! I knew they'd be here."

"How?" Jessica queries, scratching at her head and grimacing when she looks at her fingers, covered in blood.

"He remade this room from our old house. He's such a control freak and so paranoid that I figured he would have a secret compartment for weapons like he did back then." They both nod in understanding. Phoebe hands them the weapons and retrieves her gun from the corner she kicked it to earlier, checking the waistband of her leggings where the taser and knife are still hidden. Dean stares at her longingly, reaching down to adjust himself.

"Really?" Phoebe and Jessica say in unison.

"What?! It's not my fault that you look like an avenging angel Darling. Also who did you bring to help?"

"Jack, Piper and Leon." Jessica's face lights up at the mention of Piper and Phoebe makes a mental note to ask her about that when they are out of here. She cocks her gun, keeping it trained on the door as she slowly opens it, gasping as she sees bodies littering the floor. Phoebe looks at their faces, not recognising any of them. Kathy and Joel are still out there, planning god knows what. She glances back at Dean and Jessica, checking they are okay. They stare grimly at the bodies before they keep moving, stepping over the deceased. Phoebe's eyes flit about, checking every nook and cranny, gun trained on the hallway in front of them. They fall into silence as they move, and Phoebe hears someone talking on the phone in a side room. She puts her ear up to it, struggling to make out all the words.

"Yes, I can get her to you… I need to split them up… strong… together…outside?…" Phoebe shoves the door open, aims and fires three bullets into the persons chest, watching in fascination as they slam back into the wall. She closes the door and moves back to Dean and Jessica, who are watching her with morbid shock on their faces. Phoebe shrugs and moves forward, listening to the shuffling of their feet behind her.

"How did you do that so calmly?" Jessica whispers, whilst she steps in the same place Phoebe does.

"Easy, they are threatening people I love, so I'm doing what's necessary." A sharp intake of breath follows a moment of silence, then a soft groan of pain. Phoebe ignores it, knowing they need to find Joel, Kathy and the third member, who Phoebe knows is lurking around somewhere. A speaker crackles to life, and the hairs on Phoebe's arms stand on end, and she stops abruptly, causing Phoebe and Dean to bash into her back slightly.

"What's wrong Squidge?"

"Why have we stopped?" They both say simultaneously. Phoebe doesn't move; her feet rooted in place as shivers run down her spine. A soft melody runs down the hall, the sound slightly distorted but Phoebe's bottom lip quivers as she realises the song. She lets out a soft whimper, shaking her head and then turning to a camera in the corner. It swivels slowly towards her, before tilting on its axis, mocking her.

"I was… r…raped to this song… and then he played it on repeat for two days…"

"What a fucking prick" Jessica exclaims as she sticks her finger up to the camera.

"At least now we know where he is" they turn to look at her, "the control room. He's good with security and cameras, plus he likes 'control' so it makes sense that's where he would be".

"Now we just need to find it, and this place is like a maze." Dean groans, wrapping an arm around his stomach. Phoebe narrows her eyes at the movement before glancing around, then shrugging off her hoodie and yanking off the front of Dean's shirt that is somehow still held together. As it falls to the floor, her stomach rolls at the sight. A deep bleeding cut into his side, his skin already looking yellow and green in places. Jessica lets a tear out and Phoebe quickly wraps her hoodie around the bleeding wound, pulling the arms tight to hold it in place.

"Sorry" she mutters as she wipes the blood on her leggings. A gun goes off close to them and they all whirl round, Phoebe's gun drawn again. Blonde hair sticks round the corner and Phoebe's grip tightens on the trigger before she lets out a slow breath.

"Jack, you made it. How many are left?"

"Well, I'm glad to see you're all alive, there's three people left. Joel, that woman from the room these two were held in" he jerks his head towards Dean and Jessica before continuing, "though she did oddly look like Dean's therapist, and there's a man with ginger hair who kind of looks like a rat." Phoebe's eyes go wide and she takes a step backwards.

"Yes, it was the therapist. Not him as well. Fuck me sideways."

"Later Squidge... sorry not the time or place" he says before dipping his head as Phoebe pins him with a glare that could send someone to their grave.

"Okay I'm guessing we don't like him." Jessica mutters and Phoebe nods, grimacing as memories threaten to flood to the surface but she locks them back in a box, and buries them into a corner of her mind.

"Pitch. He's a dick, massive ego, may as well be Joel's evil brother. They don't look like each other but they have such similar personalities that they may have well as been." Phoebe looks around before walking towards a random room, opening the door and quickly checking it.

"Where's Piper and Leon?" Dean asks. Jack shrugs.

"Last time I saw them, they were creating chaos on the left side of the warehouse." Jack keeps an eye on Phoebe as she clears all the rooms around them, her shoulders tight and hands shaking slightly. He narrows his eyes but doesn't say anything, offering his shoulder to Dean to lean on.

"Joel won't be on the left side then. Did you see a control room or camera room whilst you were running around?" Phoebe shouts from off in the distance, popping a few shots into someone running out of a room.

"There was one a few corridors down but that door is locked tight from the inside."

"I can get us in." Phoebe sticks her head round the corner, beckoning them over. Gingerly they walk towards her, and Jack quickly takes the lead towards Joel. Dean grabs Phoebe's hand, and they walk behind Jack and Jessica as they mutter about something.

"How are you holding up Squidge?"

"I'm okay, I just want this to be over with. I can't see anyone else get hurt." Dean stares off into the distance before nodding.

"Even if that means giving yourself to him, so everyone else lives?"

"If it comes down to it again, yes, I would do it in a heartbeat if that meant I could save everyone. You have all done so much for me, I need to end this for everyone." She stares off into the hallway, wondering how everything is going to go down.

"Squidge, I can't see you get hurt from these people again."

"It won't come to that."

"How do you know?" He squeezes her hand in reassurance and protectiveness.

"I've been trained by some of the best people, plus I have barely contained rage that needs to be let out. This won't be pretty." He hums in response but says nothing further as Jack leads them around the last corner and points at a door. Phoebe walks up to it, kneels down and holds out a hand to Jessica for a bobby pin. Jessica hands it over and Phoebe pops it in, jiggling it up once, down twice and then turning it as the handle drops. She smiles at the group triumphantly, and they all give a grim smile back. Phoebe grabs her gun, checking it once over and then opens the door, aiming in front of her, finger on the trigger. A collective gasp from the group floods the room as they see Kathy hanging from the ceiling, throat slashed and stomach cut open. Jessica retches over the floor and Jack holds her hair back. Phoebe and Dean glance around the room, and find another door off to the side. They make their way over and Phoebe slowly tries the door, which to their surprise, opens with ease.

As they step inside, they instantly stop, holding their breath as Joel points a gun at the two of them. A shadow flickers in the corner and a tall man with a scraggly beard emerges, pointing a gun at Jack and Jessica as they come through the door. Phoebe's eyes flick to the man and she glares at him. He lets out a throaty chuckle.

"Damn Phoebe, you've all grown up and filled out in all the right places. God, I can't wait to be between those thighs again." His finger brushes over the trigger and Dean waits, suspension coiling around his body like a snake.

"Such a shame for you that you'll never be there again." She hisses at him, but never taking her eyes of Joel, her chest heaving and fist clenching at her side as she keeps her gun level with him. Joel flicks his eyes over to Pitch, and Phoebe sees her opening. In a rush of movement, she barrels into him and his arm goes wide as he squeezes the trigger. She stomps down on his bad leg, and he screams in pain. Phoebe's heart beats wildly in her chest and she hears the blood rushing to her ears as she shoots a bullet into his arm before straddling him.

"Never thought I'd see the day where you'd be on top Darling" he says with a sick grin and bucks his hips, trying to throw her off. Her eyes dart to Dean and Jessica, pride booming as she watches Dean pummel Pitch into the ground, Dean's face contorted in anger as he punches Pitch repeatedly. Jessica walks up to Dean, pulling him off and shaking her head. She reaches down for Dean's gun and stands over Pitch.

"This is for my best friend you piece of shit." She empties the chamber into his chest, watching as he gurgles on his own blood before going still. Relief floods her veins before she remembers Joel is still wiggling under her, groaning as he rubs his crotch against hers. Phoebe turns back to him, glaring as he licks his lips.

"It's so good to have you back in my arms. I was sceptical about leaving you alone for a few years, but that dumb bitch in there," Joel jerks his head to the room Kathy is hanging in, "but playing the long game was so much fun, and making you think that I had moved on and you had no clue that I was living in the same apartment as your boyfriend." Joel begins to laugh manically and Phoebe just tilts her head at him. She refuses to give him the satisfaction of answering, instead grabbing her knife and stabbing him. He screams in pain, feeling the knife sink into his skin repeatedly. Phoebe leans down and whispers in his ear.

"How does it feel? To be so helpless below someone, and to have other people watching this, knowing they won't help you?

How does it feel, being so close to death? Do you feel regret or calmness?" Phoebe lands a blow on his face, shaking her hand as pain radiates through the bone but does it again. She keeps going until Joel's face is barely recognisable, and her eyes widen in surprise at the damage she's inflicted. Phoebe turns to look at the group, but they nod in approval.

"Let it all out Darling" Dean says, his face screwing up in pain as he holds his side and Phoebe's heart skips a beat. Another patch of blood streams out of him and she whimpers at the fact that he got hurt again for her.

"You'll never be free of the things I've done to you", the monster below her stutters out.

"Maybe not, but at least the world will be a better place without you in it." She stands up before grabbing her gun, aiming at his head and firing. The bullet sprays blood everywhere and leaves a small hole in his head, smoke rising from it a bit. Phoebe lets out a scream of pain and releases the whole chamber into his body, it shaking with the force. Her shoulders slump, but then Jack hands over his gun, nodding towards Joel. She empties his gun too. Phoebe falls to her knees, tears streaming down her face and Jessica rushes over to her, wrapping an arm around her and letting Phoebe cry her heart out. A few minutes pass before anyone speaks.

"Bombs are in place; we need to leave now. Dean, can you walk?" Jack asks and Deans nods. They quickly make their way to the exit, and once they get a safe enough distance away from the warehouse, Jack calls Piper and Leon.

"Guys we are out, blow it." He ends the call and an almighty boom rings out across the area. They all watch in satisfaction as debris flies everywhere and shades of reds, yellows and oranges paint the sky.

Dean lets out a groan of pain, and falls to his knees, his face an ashen grey and Jack lets out a startled gasp as Dean falls on his foot.

"Fuck we need to call an ambulance" someone says nearby but Phoebe just watches helplessly as she kneels by Dean, grabbing his hand and resting her head on his forehead. His breathing grows shallow and she lets out a heart wrenching sob as she feels his chest shudder against hers.

"Dean don't you dare leave me. I can't live without you. I love you."

"About bloody time." Dean groans out before his eyes close.

"NO!" Phoebe screams, grabbing his shoulders and shaking him, sirens wail in the distance and Phoebe feels someone grabbing at her. She attempts to fight them off back strong muscular arms wrap around her, pinning her in place.

"Pheebs, it's okay, Jack and Jessica are trying as best they can until the ambulance gets here, but we need to give them space." Leon, Phoebe recognises his voice, lets out a grunt as she throws her leg back but he recovers quickly, tangling his legs with hers as he leans against a nearby tree for support. Phoebe's breath grows shallower as panic claws at the edges of her mind. Leon murmurs words of encouragement and when the ambulance finally arrives, Dean is hastily hoisted onto a stretcher and Leon finally releases her, letting her fling herself into the ambulance.

"Sorry ma'am, only family members are allowed on."

"I'm his girlfriend, now let me the fuck on before I shoot you." Phoebe had used all the bullets but they didn't need to know that. The paramedic nods quickly before letting her on, and Phoebe watches as the rest of her group run towards the car she used to get here. Phoebe attempts to stay out the way as they start running tests and trying to find the source of the bleeding.

"He was shot twice, I think, and I don't know if the bullet came out" she says with a gasp, tears flooding down her face. The paramedics stare at her in surprise and then radio ahead, letting the hospital know they have a GSW on the way and to have an OR ready. Phoebe grabs Dean hand and refuses to let go all the way to the hospital. As he flatlines, Phoebe feels like her world has come crushing down.

Chapter Thirteen

Phoebe stands like a robot as she watches Dean being wheeled off the operating room, her body as still as a statue. The sound of the wheels continues in her mind, and she reacts as the doors they entered through open forcefully, hitting the walls behind them. Phoebe whirls round to punch someone, but when they let out a shriek, she stops with her fist poised mid-air. Behind her stand Jessica, Piper, Jack and Leon, all with solemn expressions. She doesn't miss they balloons saying 'get well soon' and a massive cuddly bear that Leon looks at it as if it's the devil.

Phoebe breaks down and drops to the floor, Jessica meeting her and wrapping Phoebe in a blanket as she rubs Phoebe's shoulders. Jessica allows her to cry into her shoulder, letting her get it all out before she attempts to speak.

"Dean is going to be fine, Phoebe. He's so strong and stubborn, he wouldn't leave without saying goodbye" Phoebe throws her a look of disbelief "okay, that probably wasn't the best thing to say, but Dean loves you, he'll fight to stay here with you." Phoebe nods against her shoulder, tears streaming down her face, snot dripping from her nose. Jessica slowly brings her to stand up, flinging a bag over her shoulder, and begins leading her to the bathroom, pinning the others with a look as they attempt to follow.

"I'm going to get Phoebe changed and cleaned up. You guys wait out here and see if there are any updates." They all nod in response and Jack moves to go speak to the purple haired receptionist behind the counter.

She lightly shoves Phoebe into the toilet and Phoebe stares in shock at her reflection. Crusty blood coats her clothes and mattes her hair, some bruises blossoming on her cheeks, them already turning a blue/purple colour. She lets out a shuddering breath, watching Jessica out of the corner of her eye as she rummages around in the bag, pulling out a long sleeved top and some of Dean's trackies. Phoebe's eyes light up at the clothing but she forms when Jessica holds them out of reach.

"Sweetie, you need to get cleaned up before you put these on, you don't want to ruin his clothes do you?" Phoebe shakes her head and quickly fills up the sink with hot water and some of the hand soap, swirling it around before shrugging off her top. She quickly wipes herself dry with a towel that Jessica hands to her, hands still shaking a bit. Phoebe wets her face, wincing as she rubs on a particular sore part of her head, blood coming off and making the water a pale red. Phoebe pulls on the long sleeved top and then disregards the leggings she was wearing. Luckily, most of the blood didn't seep through the leggings so Phoebe hastily pulls on Dean's trackies, sighing in happiness. She turns to Jessica and gasps in surprise. Jessica's face looks flawless, her makeup professionally covering any bruises or cuts and Phoebe stares at her in fascination.

"What? You didn't grow up with crappy parents without figuring out how to hide bruises and stuff from the school." Jessica says, not with any real anger, but more stating facts. Phoebe just blinks at her in response, watching as Jessica grabs something from the bag and handing it to her without saying another word. The soft texture feels amazing in her hands, and as she takes in the patterns, she lets out a squeak of happiness, sitting down on the floor and pulling the fluffy socks over her feet, warmth seeping into her bones. Phoebe stands up again and shuffles towards the door, stopping as Jessica grabs her wrist.

"Phoebe, don't let Kathy sway your opinions of therapists. Not all of them are going to have a secret agenda or be scheming with an ex-fiancé." Phoebe stares at her then shakes her head, pulling her wrist out of Jessica's grip.

"I am never seeing a therapist again. I am not making that mistake for a second time." Phoebe's nose turns up at the thought, her skin breaking out in a cold sweat.

"You can't live your life hiding anymore Phoebe. I am saying this as a best friend, but you need to keeping talking to a therapist, even if Dean has to get his 'team' to do more than a background check. You are both going to need to talk about everything you have been through." Jessica gathers all of the things back into her bag, gagging slightly at the stench of dried blood.

"We can just talk to each other about it." Jessica whirls around to look at Phoebe, anger crossing her face.

"You didn't see all the things that Joel did to him or to me. We were missing for two hours before you even realised, so engrossed in your cleaning that you didn't think to check up on us. You are not Dean's therapist, just like he is not yours. The sooner you get that through your head, the better."

"You can't seriously blame me for what happened? The people to blame are all six feet under rubble now. I never saw Dean as a therapist, but quite frankly I don't trust hardly anyone not to stab me in the back, and by the looks of it, I need to take you off the list of the people I trust." A look of shame and upset crosses Jessica's features. She shakes her head and shrugs the bag onto her shoulder.

"If that's what you need to do, then so be it. But Phoebe, we have been best friends for four years, and I have been through your side through everything. I shouldn't be being pushed away just because I am voicing my opinions. I have never disagreed with anything you have said, but you know my stance on this. Unless you get the help, I won't be a big part of your life anymore. I'll still be around but not as much." Jessica opens the door, and Phoebe watches as she sits next to Piper, the latter glaring at Phoebe as she walks out of the bathroom and sits next to Jack on the other side of the room. Jack wraps his arm around her and pulls her close.

"Go to sleep Phoebe, I'll stay awake for any updates. Dean will kill me if I don't look after you." She nods against him and lets her eyes flutter close. Her breath steadies and just before she dips into sleep, she could have sworn she heard Jack speak.

"You speak like that to Phoebe again Jessica, I'll make your death look like an accident..."

A few hours later

"Phoebe wake up, Dean's out of surgery and we can go see him." Jack's voice floods her brain and she groggily opens her eyes, wiping the eye gunk from the corners and staring at him. Jack gently shakes her shoulders again and repeats himself. As the words sink in, she flings herself up and wraps Jack in a warm embrace. He chuckles softly, before pulling her in the direction of Dean's hospital room. A nurse stops them before they can open the door.

"He's awake but he's still touch and go, so be careful, he doesn't want more than two people in the room at the same time." Phoebe lets out a sob, clutching at Jack's arm for support as he takes a sharp breath in. He shakes his head, and opens the door, easing them into the room. The only sounds in the room is Dean's laboured breathing and the steady beeping of the machines. Dean watches them through half open eyes, studying them as they take in the room. Phoebe lets go of Jack's arm, and inches over to the bed, sitting on the edge of a seat placed in the corner. Dean turns to look at her.

"Wh…what are you doing over there Squidge?" he rasps out. She quickly gets up and grabs him a cup of water, helping him to drink it.

"I didn't want to sit on the bed and hurt you." She whispers, voice tight from crying so much and she blinks back tears again. She looks up at Jack and he sits on the other side of the bed, actually on the mattress, and gives Dean a side hug, careful not to put too much weight on his side.

"Glad to see you're still kicking brother, not sure how I'd run the company without you beside me." Dean laughs but then coughs a few times, his hand shaking as he reaches for the water again. Phoebe hands the water to him, looking at the mattress.

"What's wrong Squidge?"

"What do you mean what's wrong? You had to have surgery and you are in hospital because of me." She sobs softly and Dean pats the space beside him, her moving gingerly to sit next to him. Dean wraps his arm around her waist, burying his face into her side and giving her tiny kisses before looking back up at her.

"Phoebe, I would jump in front of a bullet every day for you if that meant you would live, and that I could be with you. You're it for me; there is no one else I want. You are the other half of me; it's like you were destined to be mine." Phoebe looks down at him, running her hands through his hair, causing him to groan softly in response.

"Did I hurt you?" she says as she goes to pull her hands away, but stops as Dean shakes his head.

"Nope Darling, if anything, it was the complete opposite." Phoebe lets out a soft giggle and Dean grins at the sound, before his eyes start to close. Phoebe goes to move.

"Stay Darling. I want you here with me always." She nods and together they fall asleep in each other's embrace. Neither of them notice as Jack slips out the room, stating both of them need sleep. Neither of them notice as Jack locks the door, slipping the key underneath it so they can get out but no one can get in, apart from other doctors.

Chapter Fourteen

After four gruelling days of hospital food and crappy coffee, Dean is finally released from the hospital. Phoebe and Jack help him walk out with as much assistance as they can offer.

"I'm fine, the doctors cleared me—I'll be okay walking to the car alone." Dean urges, trying to shrug out of their grip, but they each hold firm.

"Well excuse me Mr Independent, but I don't want to see you pop a stich or collapse in front of me again." Jack jokingly says, but with a firm undertone. Dean gives him a slide glare but doesn't say anything as Phoebe speaks up too. She hasn't spoken the past few days, trapped in her own head, thinking of everything but nothing.

"I agree with Jack; I think one memory of that happening is more than enough." Dean sighs but doesn't push the issue further, knowing that they both need this. The group makes it outside and Dean stands still, breathing in the spring air, allowing it to clean his lungs and fill him with a sense of peace. Jack and Phoebe let him have his moment, but then start moving him gently to his car, and opening the back door. Dean feigns mock horror.

"Oh no way am I letting either of you drive my beauty, you will certainly kill us all, as well as some innocent people."

"Hey! We are innocent people too." Phoebe gasps out, Jack nodding in agreement.

"Oh yeah, one of you hunts abusive people and 'ends' them for a living, and the other is angel who killed people who abused her. I don't think a jury would find any of us 'innocent'". Dean says matter of factly, smirking at both of them. They bristle at his words but relax slightly when they note his teasing tone and calm demeanour.

"Well tough, you ain't driving until you have bene out the hospital for a few days. Now who would you rather drive, me or the woman who hasn't actually got her licence yet." Jack states, pushing Dean into the back seat and walking to the driver's side without another word. Phoebe makes sure Dean is buckled in and then gets in the passenger side.

"What you're not going to sit back here with me?"

"Nope, I've got to control the aux since these guy here" she nods to Jack, "has disgusting taste in music. Did you know all he listens to is guys screaming?" Jack rolls his eyes and starts the car, pulling out of the parking space and starting the journey back to Dean's flat. Dean's heart beats in his chest at the fact they have spent so much time together recently, happy that Phoebe has made another friend, especially since everything between her and Jessica has transpired. The two of them have barely spoken at all, neither of them texting the other. Phoebe shuffles around a puts on a random playlist, the car flooding with violins, electric guitars and beautiful symphonies. Jack lets out a groan of protest and goes to open his mouth, his eyes glancing to Dean. He subtly shakes his head and Jacks nods in understanding. They continue the drive in quiet, letting the calmness of the music wash over them.

As Jack turns into the parking area for the apartment, both Dean and Phoebe's heart catches in their chest, their breathing becoming laboured. Jack eyes them both warily, parking the car but leaving the engine running.

"Guys, are you okay?" He asks gently and looks at both of them. They shake their heads. He lets out a small breath.

"Is it being back here?" They nod. *Okay, not speaking but communicating,* Jack thinks, *I can work with this.*

"Do you both feel safe?" they shake their heads, sweat dripping down their foreheads and Jack notes that Dean clenches his fists resting on his lap.

"Shall we leave? Go get coffee and food?" They nod. He hums in response, releases the handbrake and drives to a McDonalds, on the other side of the city, putting as much space as they can between them and the flat.

By the time they get there, a few hours has passed as lunch time rush hour traffic had been a menace. Jack orders for all of them, knowing Dean and Phoebe won't have the strength to talk. Jack grabs the food from the window and pulls into a parking space, killing the engine and handing out drinks and food. Phoebe grabs her chicken wrap and coke, eating and drinking slowly, as if savouring every bite. Dean chows through his burger, leaving crumbs over the seat and looking frustrated at himself with the mess.

"It's fine, I'll get Leon to clean it up later." Dean grunts in response. Phoebe and Dean munch quietly and once they are both finished, they breath out a sigh of relief at their full stomachs. Jack attempts to test the water, seeing if he can get them to open up.

"Do you guys think you can go back there?" They look at each other in the mirror before Phoebe lets out a shaky breath.

"No, I honestly don't think we can."

"I think we should look for another place to live." They both say in unison, smiling gently at each other. Jack nods, but lets them continue to speak, Dean taking the lead.

"I'm going to have a look and get in contact with a few people who owe me favours and see if there's anything on the market right now. What sort of things should we look for?" Dean aims his last question at Phoebe and she takes a slurp of her drink, pondering it.

"I think at least 3 bedrooms, one for us and one for guests, the other can be a little library for all our books. Oh and a decent sized kitchen for cooking and a coffee bar." Dean makes a note in his phone and then slowly steps out of the car, phoning people. Jack and Phoebe sit in comfortable silence, waiting for Dean to return. He slowly gets into the car, looking nervous as he glances at both of them.

"Well what's the verdict?" Jack says, tracing the stiches of the steering wheel.

"There's a friend of mine, she is in real estate, and she has a house close by that we can go and view today." Jack nods but Phoebe looks unsure.

"Surely, it's a bit last minute, and I don't want to put your back out Jack."

"Nah it's fine, I figured today might be difficult so I cleared my schedule, if you guys want to go look at the house then that's fine. What's the address Dean?" He quickly gets Phoebe to pop it into her phone, not wanting to mess up with the music. They drive to the house, taking them about twenty minutes, the trio chattering about pointless stuff.

Jack turns down a little off road track, all of their eyes going wide as they take in the house in front of them. A deep red converted barn stares at them, with a silver car parked out the front. Rose bushes creep up the sides of the barn and flowers decorate the garden. Phoebe breathes in at the sight and casts her gaze back to Dean, who offers a small smile. Jack parks up once more and they clamber out as a woman with brown hair, an hourglass figure and piercing blue eyes steps out the front door.

"Dean, darling, how good to see you! It's been way too long", the woman exclaims and embraces him gently, before turning to Jack, "and you, you promised you would keep in contact!". Jack mutters something under his breath, and Phoebe watches the interaction with confusion.

"Diana, lovely to see you. Apologies I haven't spoken to you in the past few months, we've been a bit busy lately. Phoebe," he turns to look at her, "this is my friend Diana, I helped her out of a horrible… situation once, and managed to help get her started in real estate."

"Oh don't beat around the bush Dean. My husband used to beat me every day, and when he laid a hand on my child, I knew I had to get out of there. A friend of mine told me about Dean, I reached out, and here we are." Diana explains, before clapping her hands, not dwindling on the past.

"Right, shall I give you guys a tour?" They all nod in agreement and walk into the house. Light blue walls make the space seem brighter, and Dean instantly starts checking the walls for any signs of leaks, when happy he comes back and grabs Phoebe's hand.

Together they explore the house as Diana talks about the maintenance history and any potential issues that may arise. High ceilings and big windows create an airy atmosphere, with love seats by the windows. They walk into the kitchen, eyes growing wide as they take in massive cooker off the side of the kitchen, and the island in centre. Phoebe runs her hands along the marble countertop, feeling the coolness beneath her skin making her shiver slightly. The rustic brown cupboards stand out against the cream tiles of the kitchen, and Dean stares at it longingly, thoughts of cooking Phoebe meals and having a coffee bar flood his brain. Phoebe watches him attentively and shares a knowing look with Jack. They move into the living room which has an alcove for a fireplace, and enough space for a few sofas. Phoebe's heart fills with happiness at the thought of her and Dean hanging out in the evenings, and having their friends over.

Diana shows them around the bedrooms, each with an ensuite and space for a bed, desk and multiple chest of drawers. All of them are on the first floor, a reasonable distance between each other but not too far. A long hallway separates them, with gold details decorating the walls.

"When you and Jessica start talking again, this would be a good room for her to stay in, don't you think?" Dean says as they take in the soft gray walls and wooden flooring. Phoebe lets out a huff at his comment, Jack laughing slightly from behind them.

"I'm not sure if we will ever speak again, to be honest with you, and it might be for the best. She did sacrifice a lot for me, and was always there for me when I would have my anxiety or PTSD attacks." Phoebe sighs but carries on looking around the room, images of a nursery flooding her brain and she shivers at the thought, unsure if she would like kids or not.

"Never say never Darling. Also, what do you think of this maybe being a nursery one day?" Dean looks over at her, feeling her hand tremble slightly in his. She shrugs and Dean decides not to push the subject.

"What do you guys think then?" Jack asks as he leans against the doorframe, watching intently. Dean and Phoebe twirl to look at him, both with happiness flooding their faces. They glance at each other, nodding slightly.

"I think it would make a lovely home after everything that has transpired." Dean states, looking around the room again before they start moving out and down the winding stairs, finding Diana in the main entrance, talking to another couple.

"Yes, we are very interested in this property…" Dean cuts them off.

"Diana, I don't think it's necessary to show these lovely people around. Whatever the asking price is for the house, double it and that's what I'll pay for it." The couple looks distraught, the man's face pulling into a tight grimace, but Diana just nods her head before escorting the couple out, shutting the door behind them.

"That won't be necessary Dean. When I saw that you and Phoebe were interested in this house, I started filling out the paperwork for you. I just had to show that couple at least the entrance way so I didn't get in trouble with my boss." Dean looks at Diana in surprise.

"How did you know myself and Phoebe were interested?"

"It wasn't so much interested, but more that I can see you living here for a while, and you both seem at peace here. Heaven knows you need it after everything you have been through, the pair of you." She looks at Phoebe gently, but Phoebe avoids her gaze, staring down at Dean's hand intertwined with hers. She squeezes it in response, running her thumb along the side of his hand.

"How much for this place Diana?" Dean questions, grabbing his cheque book from his pocket, rummaging around for a pen. Jack grabs one from his jeans, but Diana flaps her hands, shooing him away.

"Nothing, consider my debt owed." Diana pins Dean with a look, Phoebe shuffling uncomfortably in her spot.

"It was never a debt Diana." He says sympathetically, shaking his head, a few strands of hair falling in front of his eyes.

"'Then accept it as a gift for your girlfriend".

"Oh they haven't actually asked each other yet", Jack says wickedly, smiling like a kid in a toy shop. Diana lets out a gasp of shock before glaring at Dean, but the corner of her mouth turns up teasingly.

"To be honest, I thought we were together after the whole 'almost dying part'". Dean says laughing, gently squeezing Phoebe's hand before turning to look at her. Tears fill her eyes as he tilts her head up with a light grip on her chin, his other hand brushing her tears away.

"Do you want to be my girlfriend Phoebe?" Dean whispers.

"Yes, more than anything. I fought for so long, trying to keep us apart, but no more. I love you Dean, and I want to live in our own place, with no memories, so we can create new ones." Phoebe states lovingly, her heart hammering in her chest as she watches his face. Dean reaches out a hand and Diana places the key in his hand, before then slowly moving to Phoebe. Diana gently opens her hand, being wary as Phoebe flinches, and places a second one in her palm. Phoebe clenches it in her fist, then reaches up and bumps her nose against Deans, smiling softly.

"I suppose we better get another copy for Jack", Dean casts a look over to his best friend, nodding slightly and flashing him a cheeky grin.

"I bloody hope so buddy, I don't have anyone else to steal snacks from." Jack laughs and hugs Diana goodbye, opening the door for Phoebe and Dean. They hug Diana as well but Phoebe lingers behind as the men talk, heading up towards the car.

"Can I ask you a question Diana? I'm sorry if it comes off as personal." Phoebe asks quietly as Diana stands still next to her.

"Of course Sweetie, I'm pretty open about what I went through." She says cheerfully.

"How long did it take for you to feel 'okay'?" Phoebe runs a hand through her hair, remembering what Jessica said in the hospital.

"I don't think I'll every be 'okay' with what happened, but I've learnt to accept that's part of my past. But the best thing I did, was get the help I needed, and being around friends and people I knew cared about me, like my son."

"How long did it take you to reach out to some friends and to start therapy?"

"It took me a while but I wish I had reached out sooner. But I understand your hesitation with the therapist side, but I can assure they are not all like that." A flicker of doubt crosses Phoebe's face, her wondering if she did the right thing by disagreeing with Jessica.

"Maybe one day I'll do it, but I can't right now, I just want to focus on me and Dean."

"True and also normal, but you can't ignore the past, but you can learn from it." Phoebe's lips quirk up at the Lion King reference, her mind flashing back to her dad watching it on the television when she was younger. Jessica pats her arm calmly.

"Go to him, heal, love, be kind, but most importantly, fall in love with yourself again." Diana smiles again, and walks away, getting in her car and driving off. Phoebe releases a slow breath before joining the men in the car, sitting in the back as the two of them talk up front together. She leans her head against the window and the car starts, quickly lulling her into a soft slumber.

Chapter Fifteen

The final box for house was finally unpacked after a couple months, Phoebe setting down the coasters on the dining room table she and Dean had picked up after a trip to Ikea. She stands in the archway of the dining room, taking in the dark orange walls and hardwood floor. Glasses and mugs stand on the table, with a vase full of Lillies and Tulips in the centre. Warm hands rest on her waist and Dean rests his head in the crook of her neck.

"Morning Squidge, how are you feeling?" He says, voice muffled and Phoebe giggles slightly as his breath tickles her ear.

"Morning Teddy, I am tired but okay, just taking in everything. Are you okay? I noticed you didn't sleep well." She says in awe, mentioning his nickname and he grins against her skin. The nickname came about a few months ago, when they were lying in bed and Phoebe likened him to a cuddly teddy. From that moment on, that was Dean's nickname between them.

"Glad you're okay, and I'm okay Darling. What's on the agenda for today?"

"I've got my therapist appointment in a few hours but other than that I don't think there's anything planned. Is there something you would like to do?" She says before kissing the top of his head as she feels him nod in her neck. Dean raises his head to look at her, his dark stormy eyes swirling and a mischievous smile painting his lips.

"Oh god, what have you done?" Phoebe grins back, secretly loving it when Dean surprises her.

"Jessica is coming over after your therapy session, so I thought we could do something beforehand if you'd like?" Dean keeps his arms around her, but as Phoebe attempts to wriggle free, he lets her shrug him off.

"Excuse me? Why is she coming over?" Phoebe says with a glare, crossing her arms over her chest and moving further into the dining room.

"Because she reached out to me and wanted to come over and see our place since we are now settled in." She looks at him in disbelief, mostly because he didn't tell her.

"Are we just ignoring the fact that she abandoned me when I needed her the most?" Tears brimming her eyes, and she wipes them away angrily.

"No, we are not ignoring it, that's one of the things we have spoken about." Dean says slowly, taking a few tentative steps in Phoebe's direction but stopping by one of the chairs when she steps back, not wanting to overwhelm her.

"How long have you been back in contact with her?" Dean looks down at his feet, biting his lip, before meeting her stern glare again, visibly gulping at the intensity; "How long Dean? How long have you hidden this from me?" Her voice raises slowly, her temper flying through the roof before she takes a deep breath, attempting to calm herself down.

"We've been talking for the past few days, but she was the one to reach out to me, I didn't want to make the first move. Nothing has been said about you, apart from Jessica asking how you were in the first message she sent. Jessica does care about you Squidge, and I'm not going to excuse the fact that you needed her and she left without much communication, but she's here now and she wants to at least talk to you about it." Dean explains, trying to be as clear as he can, watching her closely and she struggles to process his words. In Phoebe's mind, all she sees is Jessicas back walking out of the hospital and memories of her attempting to reach out, but finding out Jessica blocked her. Heartache floods her body and she begins to shake in both fear and frustration.

"It doesn't matter Dean; you should have told me. I don't like it when you hide things from me." He stares at her, unblinking as his own trauma resurfaces, visions of his father saying the same thing to his mother as he beats her. Dean shakes his head, pulling himself out of the memory. His hand grips the chair as Phoebe continues speaking, and he listens to every word and her tone, knowing he messed up by not telling her and she feels lied to.

"What if I didn't want to speak to her? How would that situation have gone down? By not telling me, you have made me feel insignificant and as if it doesn't matter my thoughts on this."

Phoebe rambles, wringing her hands and pacing along the floor, her eyes wild and panicked.

"But do you want to speak to her?" He asks, keeping his tone calm and even, not wanting the situation to escalate further.

"What?" She stops pacing, looking at him in confusion.

"You said 'if I didn't want to speak to her', so that gives me the impression that you do want to?"

"Of course I want to speak to her, but I wanted to decide when. I'm not sure if I'm ready to forgive her just yet. Dean, she just walked out of my life so easily, like she didn't care." Tears finally burst from her eyes and she drops to her knees as she feels the weight of the decision pressing down on her back. Dean instantly drops next to her, wrapping his arms around her and kissing the top of her head.

"I know you won't be able to forgive her just yet Darling, but I know you miss her and she was like a sister to you. But before you rescued us, some stuff happened to Jessica, stuff she didn't want to tell you as that was her trauma to deal with. I'm not saying to forgive her, but maybe try to understand that we were missing for two hours, and a lot happened in that time. There are things that happened to me that I don't talk to anyone about other than my therapist and sometimes Jack." Phoebe latches onto every word Dean utters, nodding gently in his arms.

"I'm sorry I got so upset and started shouting."

"We can work on that, I'm not going to say it's okay because it's not but we will work through it. I am sorry for not telling you about Jessica, but I'm not sorry that she reached out. As much as I love your new group of friends, I know you miss your best friend, and to be honest with you, I miss her too." Phoebe hears the sincerity in his words, and her heart breaks a little for him.

"Fine, yeah okay, let's do it, but maybe an hour or so after the therapy session, because I'll need to process everything we spoke about and I don't want that to effect the conversation with Jessica." She agrees, going to wipe the tears away from her eyes but Dean beats her to it, using the pads of his thumbs to get rid of them. He kisses the top of her head again before speaking.

"I'm proud of you Darling, this is a big step. But how about we go and do something before your therapy session, that way hopefully you won't feel anxious and maybe open up to her a bit more?" Phoebe nods again, and Dean helps her to her feet, catching her as she wobbles and steadying her. Phoebe mutters a small thank you before moving to grab her shoes, her yellow dress flowing at her knees as she walks. Dean watches her as she moves, his eyes lingering on her behind as she bends down, and she throws a small smile over her shoulder at him.

"What would you like to do Darling?" Phoebe glances over at the clock hanging on the wall as she ties her white vans onto her feet. Dean had bought her some new ones a week ago and she absolutely loves them.

"Hmm, well it's nearly 12 o'clock so maybe we could go for lunch?"

"Want to try that new Greek place?" Phoebe beams at him and nods quickly, causing Dean to let out a chuckle at her excitement. Phoebe finishes tying her laces and Dean grabs her hand with one of his and his car keys with the other. He laughs to himself and Phoebe looks over with a twinkle in her eye.

"What's so funny?"

"I was just thinking back to when Jack tried to teach you how to drive the other day."

"Hey! The curb got in my way." She laughs along with him as they walk out the house, lock the door and head towards the car parked in the drive.

"It's fine Darling, not everyone is built to be behind the wheel. Plus, I'm not complaining, you look good as my passenger princess." She giggles and nods before Dean opens the door, bowing slightly as she steps in. He walks round to the other side and quickly gets in before driving off to the restaurant.

They sit in the quiet, listening to the music softly coming from the speakers of the car, both lost in their own world. Dean turns a corner and the sign for *'The Hungry Spartan'* comes into view. The white and blue building stands out against the boring brown bricks of the London landscape. Phoebe bounces slightly in the seat and Dean smiles gently at her before turning into the car park at the back of the restaurant. They park and quickly get out, anticipation coursing through the pair of them as they walk hand in hand to the entrance. Wafts of feta, kleftiko, keftedes and tzatziki floods their noses as they open the door and a server greets them before guiding them to a table in the corner. The stone walls stand out against the rustic wooden furniture, but it all adds to the charm of the restaurant. The ceiling has exposed beams and Phoebe hums in fascination at the resemblance to an authentic Greek restaurant.

"Would you like anything to drink?" The server asks, his eyes fliting between the pair of them as they take their seats and they browse the menu.

"Can we both have a Soumada please?" Dean asks, looking over at Phoebe and she nods in approval. The server nods and heads over to the bar, pouring them both a glass from a bottle before dropping a few ice cubes into the glasses. The server heads over and places the drinks on the table before moving off to the side, giving them a chance to decide on the menu.

"What would you like Darling?" Dean says, as he places his menu down, his decision already made as he takes a sip of the alcohol-free beverage.

"I think I'm going to try the Lamb Kleftiko, I've always wanted to." Dean nods and the server comes over, sensing that they have both reached a decision.

"What can I get for you?" he asks politely.

"I'd like the Lamb Kleftiko for my girlfriend please, and I'd like to have the Keftedes please." The server nods, removes the menus and walks towards the kitchen. Dean and Phoebe sit in peaceful silence again, looking around at the restaurant and just enjoying each other's company. About twenty minutes later, the door to the kitchen opens and the server carries out two steaming hot plates, and pops them onto the table.

"I hope you enjoy your food and let me know if there's anything I can do to help elevate your dining experience here at '*The Hungry*

Spartan'." He then walks away, leaving Dean and Phoebe alone. They both look down at their plates, their mouths watering at the sight of the food in front of them. Dean's plate holds a dozen or so meatballs, served with pitta bread and a slice of lemon. Phoebe's plate holds the leg of lamb and some roasted potatoes, the smell of onions, herbs and garlic making her stomach rumble in hunger. They both pick up their cutlery and dig in, moaning in happiness and satisfaction. The meat falls apart in their mouths, and the juices flood from the meat. They eat in silence, the only sounds being cutlery clinking against the plates and the glasses being put back onto the table after taking a drink. When they finally finish, they lean back in their chairs, patting their stomachs at the same time before laughing at the fact they are in sync.

"How was your food Darling?" Dean says as he wipes his mouth with a napkin, before starting to stack the plates, ready for the server to come and collect.

"It was amazing Dean; I really enjoyed it. I'd love to go to Greece at some point as I've never been abroad." Dean's eyes twinkle in response and he gets up to pay for the food, but Phoebe beats him to it. The look of disbelief on Dean's face is priceless and Phoebe laughs in response as they get up from their seats, tucking their chairs under the table.

"Why did you pay?" Dean asks as he grabs her hand once more, needing to be close to her.

"Because I can." Pheobe responds matter of factly, squeezing his hand in response and they both nod to the server on the way out. They get into Dean's car and he heads towards the building where Phoebe's therapy session takes place. It doesn't take them long, and soon enough Dean is leaning over the centre console and gives her a peck on the cheek, after parking the car in the drop off zone.

"Have a good session Darling, and I'll be back in an hour to pick you up. I'm going to go to the shops to grab some stuff for dinner whilst you're in there. I love you Squidge." Phoebe smiles and grabs the car handle, opening the door as she looks at Dean.

"I love you too Dean, and I'll see you later." With that, she steps out of the car and walks towards the building, Dean watching as she safely goes inside, nodding to himself and driving out of the parking space.

Chapter Sixteen

P hoebe walks into the building, anxiety in her veins but her stomach full of food so she bottles down the panic as she takes a seat in the waiting room. She takes a deep breath in and then releases it slowly, calming her pounding heart as she attempts to clear her head. It is still reeling after the news that she is going to be seeing Jessica after so long. Her leg bounces up and down but Phoebe doesn't attempt to stop it, knowing that physical factor of her anxiety can't be helped. She stares at the dark red walls, her eyes fliting between some of the art pieces on the wall, but none really catching her attention as usual.

A woman with dark blue hair and light blue eyes pokes out her head from an office to the side of the hallway.

"Hi Phoebe, would you like to come in?" She smiles at Phoebe as she rises from her seat, stuffing her phone into the pocket of her dress before walking over. The door is held open and Phoebe reads the sign on it, even though she knows Doctor Theo's name by now, although she insists Phoebe calls her by her first name, Andie. Phoebe shuts the door behind her, and moves to sit in the chair by the window, waiting for Andie to open up the conversation.

"How are you doing today Phoebe? I noticed your leg bouncing as I stuck my head out." Andie says, a notepad placed on her dark wooden desk as she leans back in her chair, arms resting on the sides of it. Phoebe lets out a sigh before starting to talk.

"I am meeting Jessica today after this session and I am unsure how everything is going to play out. We haven't spoken in months and I'm anxious about screwing up I guess, and perhaps not being taken seriously." She states, still looking out the window, her finger tapping on the windowsill absentmindedly. There's a moment of silence as Andi ponders over her statement.

"Jessica. She used to be your best friend didn't she?"

"I think she still is. Yes I have made new friends like we discussed a few months ago, but she still holds a special place in my heart. I'm still battling with how everything played out between us, and I said to Dean earlier, that I'm not sure if I'm ready to forgive her just yet." Phoebe glances at Andie, trying to gauge her reaction but she keeps her expression neutral as she nods in response

"I think that's understandable to feel that unease and frustration, especially if this has just been sprung on you." Andie states, making a small note in her notebook before placing the pen down on the desk, just to the left of it. She frowns and moves it a bit further left before nodding at the placement and looking back to Phoebe who watches the movement with no judgement, but rather in fascination.

"Yes, Dean told me this morning which I didn't really appreciate as I've had no time to prepare what I'm going to say, which has made me feel quite anxious and worried, because what if I say the wrong thing and offend her, and she walks out again?" Phoebe rambles, tapping her fingers on the windowsill a bit quicker, her breath coming out in short gasps. Andie rises from her seat and stands in front of Phoebe.

"What's five things you can see Phoebe?"

"The sky," her eyes move around the room, "a desk, a bookshelf, your pen and a cushion."

"Four things you can touch?" Phoebe runs a hand over her dress as she tries to calm her breathing.

"The windowsill, the chair, my dress and my thigh."

"Three things you can hear?" Andie watches her intently, noting any signs of distress.

"Your voice, the cars outside and someone outside the door."

"Two things you can smell?" Phoebe pauses; concentration etched onto her face as she takes a breath in.

"Petrol and books." She smiles, thinking of Dean.

"One thing you can taste?"

"My food from lunch."

"Good, how do you feel now? And what did you have for lunch?" Andie asks, noting that Phoebe's breath has evened out and her leg has stopped bouncing. She smooths out her dress once more and stops tapping on the windowsill.

"Me and Dean went for lunch at that new Greek place I was telling you about last session. It was amazing and I think I'd like to go back there again soon."

"That's good to hear Phoebe, I'm glad you are trying new things, that is very good progress. How do you feel about talking through the situation with Jessica? What do you think would help you tackle this situation in a healthy way?" Phoebe turns back to the window, watching as cars slowly trickle by and she spots Dean a few shops down, bags in his hands and looking a bit lost. She smiles softly before catching Andie's gaze.

"I'm not sure, maybe... making a list of a few things... that I want to address...?" The uncertainty comes back into her voice, her tone shaking as she stumbles over her words.

"That might be helpful, that way you can make sure you stay on the right path, and not shoot down one that is completely unrelated. Would you like to work on a list together this session or is there something else playing on your mind that we should discuss?" Andie moves to sit behind her desk again, crossing one leg over the other and picking up her pen, balancing it between her fingertips.

"I like that idea, there is something else but I don't think I need to talk about it today, I think it'll still be an issue next session, whereas this meeting with Jessica is today." Andie nods and gestures to Phoebe to begin.

"I think I'd like to discuss the whole downfall of the friendship, and everything that transpired at the hospital?" Phoebe looks at Andie for confirmation and she tilts her head slightly.

"I think that is an okay idea, I'm not saying it's awful, but perhaps it would be more efficient to tell her how you felt. Rather than attacking her, try and explain how you felt in that particular moment." Phoebe bites her lip, eyebrows furrowing as her shoulders tighten.

"I don't know how to do that without people thinking I am being mean or rude or selfish. This has been an issue with everyone, including my parents and Dean sometimes." She huffs out, frustration bubbling under her skin and she rubs her hands together to calm herself down. Andie makes a quick note in her book, before taking a sip of her water on the side, a separate little side desk just for her drinks to go on. Phoebe looks at the array of drinks, water for hydration, coffee for fuel and a Fanta as Andie's 'fun' drink. All of them are meticulously placed in separate spots on the desks and Phoebe wishes she has that level of organisation.

"Okay, that's understandable and I can see how that might be stressful with trying to convey how you're feeling. How about we go through the list of emotions we made the other day and I'll bring up a situation you have told me about, and then you point to the emotion you feel the most, and then we can write a little paragraph about why you are feeling that emotion and how we can possibly help you move forward?" Phoebe nods, gets up and walks over to the side of the room, finding the emotion board mounted on the wall.

"Okay, Jessica. How do you feel about her?" Phoebe points to the unsure part of the wall, but also leans over to the angry side.

Andie nods, making a note on a big sheet of paper for Phoebe to take with her.

"And why do you feel those emotions?"

"Because I don't know if anything is going to change, and I'm angry that it got to the point we had to have so long apart, when we could have spoken about whatever was bothering her, but instead, she walked away because it was the easy option, she didn't want to put in the hard work!" Phoebe ends up ranting, her voice rising and she winces at the pain in her ear, still lingering from firing a gun so many times now. Andie nods and makes another note.

"Okay, I've written down what you said but in a clearer manner. How do you feel about being friends with Jessica again potentially?" Phoebe points to the happy section.

"How do you feel about Dean?" She gestures to the love and peace section before smiling a bit. Andie smiles back at her and continues scribbling on the bit of paper.

"Now, what about Joel? How do you feel about him after he mysteriously passed away?"

"There isn't enough emotions to describe how I feel." Phoebe rolls her eyes and picks at the skin around her nails.

"Which one do you feel the most?"

"I feel all of them, all the time. I'm happy he's gone, then I'm sad, then I'm angry, then I feel peaceful. I thought after he died, that maybe I would find more peace and be able to live my life, but I can't because I'm still getting the nightmares!" Phoebe screams, tears bursting and streaming down her face.

"But you're flashbacks are less frequent and you've made a bunch of new friends. That's an improvement Phoebe. You've only been doing this for a few months, and the healing process does take longer sometimes, even if you follow all of the right steps. Just like there is no time frame on grief, there's no time frame on healing. Perhaps that is something you can discuss with Jessica as well, maybe she needs a slight reminder?" Phoebe closes her eyes, breathing in, counts to five and then releases the breath slowly. She repeats this a few times before opening her eyes and moving away from the emotion board, sitting in the chair closest to the desk as Andie turns the paper towards Phoebe, allowing her to read over the notes. Phoebe quickly skim reads before glancing up at the clock, gasping as she realises the time.

"Yes, it's the end of our session, don't worry about the time going over, that was my own fault, so you won't get charged any extra. I'll see you next time Phoebe, and we will discuss the after math of your conversation with Jessica". Phoebe nods, grabs the paper and without uttering a word, she walks out the office, finding Dean already waiting in the reception. She squeals and runs to him, wrapping her legs around his waist as she peppers his face with kisses, him laughing in response.

"You doing better now Darling?" She nods into his neck and Dean carries her out to the car and opens the door with one hand. Phoebe unravels herself from his embrace and sits on the seat. Once Dean is in the car and reversing out of the parking spot, she turns to him.

"I'm sorry I had a go at you and got so upset. Me and Andie went through it today and we came up with a list of things to talk about, to make sure that I don't get sidetracked." Dean glances over and smiles softly, adoration flooding his face.

"Thank you for apologising and I am sorry I hid this from you. I truly think this is a good thing and I hope that maybe your friendship can start to rekindle." Phoebe hums in response and they sit in silence for the rest of the drive home.

Chapter Seventeen

Phoebe and Dean walk into the house, hands intertwined, a peaceful silence over them. Dean pulls Phoebe into the kitchen, gently pinning her against the island in the centre of the room. She lets out a soft gasp her hands fly up to grab onto his arms. Dean's head dips down and he kisses her gently, running his hands through her hair. Phoebe deepens the kiss and groans into his mouth, swiping her tongue along his bottom lip. Dean opens and their tongues battle for dominance, but when Dean removes one hand from her hair, to grab her ass, Phoebe melts into the kiss and his arms. He thrusts his hips into hers, keeping her pinned against the island and Phoebe lets out a tiny whimper. Dean lets out a small chuckle before braking the kiss, leaning his forehead against hers.

"I am so proud of you Phoebe, I hope you know that." She smiles up at him and nods quickly, still breathless from the kiss.

"One day, I'm going to put a rock on that finger, it might not be today or in the next month, but I'll do it." Phoebe stares at him, finding his devotion so sexy and bites her lip, a small blush creeping up her cheeks.

"Don't bite that lip Squidge, you know what it does to me, and Jessica will be here soon, and I don't think she really wants to walk in on what we get up to." Phoebe giggles, before pulling out of his arms, but not before giving him a quick peck on the nose, causing him to scrunch up his face in surprise.

"I suppose we better get started on dinner then, although I'm not sure what to make."

"How about we just order a pizza or three, just like you guys used to do in the old days?" Dean stares at her quizzically, as she ponders the idea, moving around the kitchen and living areas, picking up the various plates and glasses scattered around. Once she loads the dishwasher, she turns back to Dean, leaning against the counter before speaking.

"I think that's a good idea, but I think I am going to have something different today, just because I have to meet Jack tomorrow morning for our training session." She smiles happily, her eyes sparkling at the thought of channelling some of her rage into the right thing.

"Ah yes I forgot about that, how's that coming along?" Dean asks as he pulls out his phone, loading up the delivery app and sliding it across to Phoebe.

"Well, Jack's teaching me about stealth and how to get out of situations, without blowing anything up or setting anything on fire." Dean chuckles and moves to stand behind her, wrapping his arms around her waist and nuzzling his face into her neck.

Phoebes fingers slide across the phone, picking chicken tenders and a small chicken pizza.

"What would you like Teddy?" He grins into her neck, before unwrapping one of his hands and tapping two large pepperoni pizzas into the order, one for himself and one for Jessica, remembering that is her favourite. Phoebe hits the place order button, just as a message comes through from Jessica.

Jessica: Hey Dean! I'm about 5 minutes away, see you both soon. Dean nods into Phoebe's neck to respond to her, refusing to let her go as he cuddles and gently kisses her neck.

Dean: Hey Jessica, it's Phoebe. Looking forward to seeing you, we have just ordered food.

Jessica: Hi Pheebs, fabulous, I'm ravenous, better be pizza!

Phoebe lets out a small laugh at her response and places Dean's phone back on the island, her hand shaking slightly, just as the doorbell rings. Dean grudgingly releases Phoebe and huffs as he walks to the door, Phoebe's feet rooted to the floor as she tries to calm her breathing.

Slowly she calms down, and moves into the living room, sitting in her beige armchair by the window, with her iPad set up on the little table in the corner. She glances at it briefly, hey eyes flicking across the various sections of the house. Dean had set up a high level surveillance, after a particularly bad PTSD attack, where they both thought that someone was in the house. Now, they can see all of the inside and the garden, thanks to Jack helping them. Phoebe scans the different sections and watches as Dean and Jessica greet each other with a warm embrace. A bit of jealousy boils under her skin, but she tamps it down, remembering that Jessica is very much gay, and follows their movements as they walk towards the kitchen. Phoebe holds her breath, waiting for anything to happen, but what she doesn't expect, is Jessica running up to her and hugging her tightly.

"Phoebe! Oh My God, it's been so long! Look at you, you've gotten so strong and your hair, it's so thick now!" Jessica all but screams in her ear and Phoebe flinches away a bit, the noise making her ears ring, as she still suffers from the gunshots that she fired into Joel.

"Yeah Jessica, it's been a while, a lot has changed." Phoebe says as she moves away from Jessica, sitting back in her chair, the bricks around her heart slowly going back up. Dean walks over to Phoebe, perching himself on the arm, running a hand over her shoulder, squeezing gently. Jessica's smile falters for a second, but she still sits on the carpet happily and gives them the rundown of her life after the past few months of not talking.

"So me and Piper have started seeing each other. There's a lot of things that need to be worked out, but we are both willing to try," she glances over at Phoebe briefly before looking back down at the carpet as she rambles on; "we are taking things slow for now, seeing each other once a week or once every fortnight. But so far, it's going really well." Phoebe and Dean exchange curious looks before looking back at Jessica.

"How long have you been dating?" Dean asks, his fingers squeezing harder on phoebe's shoulders but when she lets out a little whimper of pain, he instantly stops.

"About a week or so after you were released from hospital." Jessica says sheepishly, brushing one of her blonde locks out of her face, looking up at them anxiously. They both take a sharp intake, annoyance slamming into Phoebe.

"So whilst we were struggling with everything that happened, you were shaking it up with a woman that hardly spoke to us, and then you walked out of our lives for months."

"I get why you're mad, I really do, but I was hurting to. That doesn't excuse how I handled things but I think at the time, that's what I needed." Jessica explains, keeping her volume the same, despite the frustration that she is feeling too. Phoebe pulls out the list that her and Andie made, smoothing it out on her legs, before looking back at Jessica.

"What's that? Reasons why I'm a bad best friend?" Jessica says, with a tinge of fear in her voice.

"No, I wouldn't be that person. But I don't think you truly understand how much I was hurt by you. But the first point on here, is me saying I'm sorry. I am sorry that you felt you had to leave the friendship because I wouldn't listen to you and I am sorry that I put you in that situation, it should never have happened." Jessica nods along, her eyes already full of tears, before she gestures to the rest of the list, ready to listen and learn.

"You knew I have abandonment issues, and yet you still walked out. Rather than talking to me about what was bothering you, you took the easy way out. I needed my best friend whilst the love of my life was in the operating room, and you didn't seem to care. You instantly ran off into the arms of another person. It seemed at the time, that you blamed me for everything that happened and that I dragged you into all of my fucked up shit." Phoebe releases a slow breath after rambling, tapping her finger on her leg, before continuing.

"You didn't give me a chance to process everything that had happened. You knew that bitch Kathy had fucked over my perception of therapists, and at that moment, I never wanted to see another one again, but I did. It took me a few weeks, but I got there, but you weren't there to see it." Phoebe sits back in the chair, noticing that she had started leaning forward, and she risks a glance at Jessica, who now has tears streaming down her face.

"Phoebe, I am sorry with how I handled everything at the time, I truly am. But I won't apologise that I needed space to deal with everything too. I think I was just frustrated because I knew that you would need professional help, and if this," she gestures between them, "is to become a friendship again, I really would like you to continue with the therapy, because I can tell it's helping. When me and Dean were with Joel, things happened, things that I am not quite ready to share just yet, but it fucked me over too, and I'm still dealing with everything that transpired. I want this friendship to work but I can't be your therapist again. I am happy for you to rant to me about things, as long as you talk to a professional as well." Phoebe listens attentively, noting the honesty in Jesscia's voice, feeling the bricks around her heart come crumbling down. She almost forgets that Dean is there until he speaks up.

"I am glad that you both are happy to work on the friendship, but Jessica, if you ever hurt Phoebe like that again, I will make your life a living hell, and you know I can." The doorbell sounds in the distance, and he gets up, leaving without a word. Phoebe and Jessica glance at each other and then burst out laughing, tears streaming down their faces.

"Well at least I know where he stands with me." Jessica laughs, wiping the tears away from her eyes.

"He's very protective of me, more than he was, but he means well." Phoebe says, and she hears Dean's shoes across the floor, the waft of pizza and chicken flooding the living room, and both women audibly groan and the stomachs let out almighty rumbles, causing them to laugh again. Dean places the food on the floor, and they all sit down, stuffing their faces like old times.

Chapter Eighteen

Phoebe and Dean are sitting at the table at the house about six months later, eating breakfast but not talking. Phoebe huffs as she pushes her croissant around on the plate whilst Dean flicks through the news app on his phone. He looks up at her briefly but doesn't say anything as he stands and heads to the bedroom, Phoebe's eyes following him like a hawk.

"Oh so you're just going to ignore what happened last night and pretend nothing happened?", she says angrily, pushing her plate away and stomping after him. He lets out a sigh and calmly walks over to the wardrobe, grabbing a work shirt and slipping his night shirt off. Phoebe's eyes run over his abs and her mouth suddenly goes very dry, but as she begins to speak again, Dean puts the shirt on and rolls the sleeves up, doing up the buttons and securing the sleeves in place.

"No I am not ignoring what has happened, but I need to get to work and I don't think it's fair on either of us to have this discussion when I need to leave. But I will say something so that you can think about it whilst I am gone, I did not appreciate what you asked of me last night. It was an impossible situation for me to be put in and I did not feel comfortable doing what you asked. From here on forward, I'd like you to respect my boundaries as much as I have respected yours." Dean grabs his suit jacket from the chair and moves to walk out.

"I do truly love you Phoebe and I would jump in front of a bullet for you. Please think about what I said and we will talk more when I'm home. I should only be gone a few hours but you know what work is like. I am not saying that to try and get out of the conversation later because it does need to happen, but I don't want to set a designated time and then potentially let you down." Dean smiles softly at her as she stares at him, seeing that she is listening to him and taking what he said on board. The flicker of upset and rejection crosses her face but she quickly shoves those emotions back into a locked box and nods at him.

He leaves without another word, and when the door closes, she collapses to her knees and cries until she can't breathe. The tightness in her chest causes her to panic and her hands shake as badly as they first did when she met Dean. She grabs her phone from her pocket and speed dials Jessica.

"Hello? Phoebe are you okay? I just got a text from Dean that you might ring..." Jessica says as she picks up after the second ring. Her brows furrow on the other end of the line as she hears Phoebe gasping for breath and the gut wrenching sobs falling through.

"Fuck it, I'm on my way over, screw work, not like they can fire me", she exclaims as she runs around to grab her bag and car keys, dashing out the door, into the car, connects the phone to her car and squeals out of the parking lot.

"It's going to be okay Phoebe, just focus on my voice and take a few deep breaths, focus on the present rather than the past", the sound of zooming cars brushes over her words as Phoebe strains to hear her voice.

"I'm not having a flashback… things aren't great between me and Dean right now. I asked him to do something last night so I could take back some of the control in my life, because despite the fact that Joel is dead, I still can't get over the shit he did to me. But when I asked Dean to do this thing, he looked at me like I had run over his cat or something", Phoebe manages to say through struggling breaths. A few moments go by as Phoebe waits for Jessica to either respond or hang up and never speak to her again. A wave of happiness washes over her as Jessica hums to herself, deliberating how to say whatever it is without hurting phoebe's feelings even more.

"Now, regardless of what it is, I am sure that Dean had his reasons for saying no, just like you had your reasons for asking for this thing to happen. Whilst you may have wanted it to take control of your life back, Dean may not have been comfortable doing that as you have only recently started going to therapy again so maybe he is not sure on how to handle the situation right now?" Jessica pulls into the apartment car park, parks somewhat okay, and walks through into the reception. The girl at the front desk notices her and nods, before zapping her through to the elevator. Jessica keeps one hand on her phone to her ear, making sure that Phoebe is on the other end of the line as the soft whirr of the elevator motor floods the eerie silence.

"Phoebe are you still there?", she asks.

"Yes, I'm just thinking about what you said and trying not to throw up", she murmurs down the phone. Her shoulders tense as a sob rake through her body, her breath hitching in her chest. The bell dings and Jessica ends the phone call as she steps through the door and rushes to Pheobe on the floor. Her hands twitch as she stares into the distance and Phoebe sits on the floor next to her, out of hand reach but close enough to stop her if needs be.

"I can't live without him, he's the air I breathe", she whispers.

"I know Sweetie, but you can't live like this. You can't be dependent on him, realistically you can only depend on one person and that's yourself. What did you and Dean fight about?" Jessica asks, as she makes sure her phone is on silent and turning it face down on the floor before nudging Phoebe gently in the shoulder. Phoebe flinches but then takes a shuttering breath, her bottom lip quivers and the words roll off her tongue.

"I asked him to... act out certain things with me... so I could take control of my life", she says hesitantly, waiting for Jessica to get up and leave like Dean did. Jessica swallows and thinks for a few seconds before speaking.

"I get how that would be able to help you potentially, but I can understand why Dean was upset that you asked him that, and I think you know as well."

"I get why it might upset but he didn't even listen to me, he just shut the idea down instantly."

"He doesn't owe you an explanation Phoebe, if he says no then that's fine. If that's a boundary that he won't cross then he doesn't need a reason to say no. Even if you think it might help you. You have to understand that you both have gone through things to do with your past." Phoebe opens her mouth to argue but Jessica quickly interrupts her.

"I am not blaming you for your past, I'll never do that again and you know it. But Dean was badly hurt and he's struggling as well. I think you both need to go back to therapy, preferably one who isn't secretly in love with you ex-fiancé, and work through your trauma, not quitting after like six months because you think you are better." Jessica never once looks away from Phoebe, maintaining eye contact and her heart thumps in her chest, her hands sweaty as she rubs them along her grey skirt as she waits for Phoebe rebuttal. Phoebe just nods and stares at the floor.

"It's going to be a hard path Phoebe, but it's not impossible to come back from this. You and Dean love each other so much and I can't imagine you guys not dating, but I think some time apart might be the best thing for you guys right now. "Jessica gets up off the floor and dials a number on her phone.

"Hi, I'd like to order two large pizzas and a side of chicken wings for delivery please", she says, grinning like a cheshire cat down at Phoebe, causing her to let out a small giggle as she slowly pulls herself off the floor and sits in her egg chair in the corner of the room, surrounded by piles and piles of books. Phoebe looks at the photo of her and Dean at the aquarium together that one of his security guards had taken. It was of her pointing at some of the fish and him looking at her with so much love in his eyes. *How did I not realise it sooner, that this man, is the love of my life,* she thought. Her eyes brim with tears as she thinks about losing Dean and how close she came to it being the truth. Her hands rub down her arms as tingles run up and down them, and she grabs a cardigan from the side, the soft fabric caressing her skin and grounding her anxiety before it can take flight. Jessica sits on the sofa to the side of Phoebe, one leg tucked under her and she fluffs her blonde hair out of her face.

"So there's a bit of a wait, given the fact it's a Saturday night, so food should be here in about an hour."

"That's okay, I'm not too hungry at the moment", Phoebe says softly, guilt encroaching into her conscious as she stares off into the distance.

"It's okay Phoebe, Dean will know that you didn't mean not too take his feelings into account. As long as you apologise and make sure it doesn't happen again then he will forgive you. But you also need to forgive yourself, not just for that but for all the hatred you have. I am not a therapist but I can see how you blame yourself for everything you've gone through and all the bad crap that's happened to your loved ones." Jessica gives her a pointed look before opening up Netflix, letting her words sink in for Phoebe, giving her the time to process the information.

They watch an episode of Supernatural, them laughing at how much Dean is like Dean, and they both jump as the door is unlocked and Dean steps through with two burning hot pizzas in his hands, smiling softly at the pair of them. He slowly walks over and places the boxes on the small coffee table, before kissing Phoebe gently on the top of the head. He takes a seat in his 'old man chair' and gestures for them to dig in. They eat in silence for a few minutes before Dean speaks up.

"I have an announcement and this couldn't have come at a better/worse time, depending on how you look at it." He pins Phoebe with a glare, causing her to squirm uncomfortably under the weight of it before turning his attention away from her.

"I am being forced to go to China to talk to some of our clients, and after that I have to go to a few other countries, those are yet to be determined. I have no idea how long I'll be gone, but maybe we can use this time wisely? I've already had a look at therapists in China and found a few highly recommended ones, perhaps we can find you one here Phoebe?" he says softly, as if not to upset her. Tears stream down her face anyway and she hiccups slightly, Dean leaning over and passing her a bottle of water.

"I'm sorry Dean, I should have taken your feelings into account, that was horrible of me, but please don't fly off to another country because of me."

"I'm not flying off to another country to be away from you, but I'm not going to argue to stay here either. I think the distance will be good for us and allow us to find ourselves again Squidge. I want to get back into a few things and perhaps you can find a hobby aside from reading." Dean lets out a soft chuckle as her nose scrunches up in disgust at the book comment before she sniffles and nods.

"How are we going to make this work and when do you leave?"

"We can call every other day or something, but I'm not losing you, you're too important to me. I'll visit as often as I can without putting my body through hell with all the time zones and work I'm going to have to do. In regard to me leaving, I go tomorrow at noon". Phoebe looks over to Jessica but she has put her headphones on and Phoebe can hear Taylor Swift blasting through the speakers. Phoebe turns back to Dean and his eyes water as he looks straight at her, before patting his lap. She gets off of the chair and pads over to him, plopping down on his lap and burrowing into his neck. Dean runs a hand through her hair and whispers sweet nothings in her ear as she lets out quiet sobs. The sound of the door opening and closing again causes Phoebe to flinch, her body jolting violently in Deans grasp.

"It's just Jessica leaving to give us some privacy", he says with a sigh, his brow furrowing at how Phoebe is going to function by herself.

"I'm going to figure out this healing shit, I promise, I'll be better for when you come home."

"I'm not asking you to be better completely Squidge, because there is no time frame that, considering how much trauma we have both endured. But I promise to try better too, as I know I failed you at times."

"In this life and every after?" She questions. His heart clenches in his chest as he grips her tightly, never wanting to let her go.

"Always darling" he responds and they both fall asleep, tangled in each other's embrace.

Chapter Nineteen

A few months later

Pheobe walks down the path from her work, a hand to her ear and a furrow in her brow. The high buildings around the city allow her a small break from the scorching summer heat. Her nose crinkles and turns at the smell of hot rubbish lining the paths, and the stench of weed billowing out of people's houses. You'd think with law enforcement kicking up a fuss about people using and selling drugs, then they'd do something about it, but not, Phoebe thought. Sweat clings to her armpits from a long day at work, and she feels the bottle of wine sitting happily in the fridge at home.

"Dean? What do you mean you have to stay out there for another few months? We haven't seen each other in ages, and I miss you", she says, the air in her lungs constricting tightly before she lets out a slow breath. Her teeth bite at her bottom lip, but she doesn't bite hard enough to bleed anymore. Her shoes beat against the ground rhythmically as she waits for Dean's reply.

"Hello? Dean, are you still there?" she asks as she checks her phone to make sure the call hasn't been disconnected. Steady breathing on the other end meets her ear, and she lets out a sigh of relief and not having to worry about calling him back.

"I'm so sorry Squidge, but I need to secure a few more deals before I can even think about coming back. I know that isn't the news you wanted to hear, and I was so ready to come home, too, but this is out of my control." Dean says with a groan at the end, genuine upset seeping through the phone to Phoebe.

"I understand that, but I just miss you. How about I find a flight to wherever you're going to be next week, and we can spend a few days together?"

"That sounds lovely, I'll have a look at tickets and get them booked for you after this call, but whilst you walk home, let's talk about anything I have missed out on", Dean says happily. They talk about anything and everything, from Jessica's new girlfriend to the latest drink at Phoebe's coffee shop.

As Phoebe turns up the road heading to her and Dean's cottage, she is chatting his ear off about their shared cat, Sir Whiskalot.

"He's gotten very cuddly over the past few days, Dean, it's as if he misses his daddy", she giggles softly. He groans in her ear, "Squidge, you know how much I hate being called the fur child's daddy. I think I am more of a cool, fun uncle that will bring it catnip and leave you to deal with it". He lets out a massive laugh as Phoebe agrees with him. Despite their earlier conversation, everything seems to be okay with them, and Phoebe lets out a breath of peace and contentment. Her eyes scan across the cottage, the roses creeping up the sides, fully in bloom as the warm breeze trickles through her hair.

"You've just seen the house, haven't you, darling?" Dean's smooth voice washes calm over her, and she hums in agreement, "No matter that we both live here, it still takes my breath away, although I see it every day". Her fingers run over the gate at the end of the garden, and gently push it open. The thatched roof stands out against the blue sky, and sun beams down on her, sweat slowly trickling down her forehead. Despite the heat and how uncomfortable it is, Phoebe looks at the house with admiration and peace.

"I wish you were here Dean, or at least I wish I was with you..."

"I know darling, but not long now till you're in my arms again."

Phoebe sighs as she opens the door, defeat slumping her shoulders and tears in her eyes as she blinks them away. It's not a big deal, she tells herself. As she walks across the wooden floor, her sneakers patter softly and she admires the dark mahogany furniture, and the high ceilings of the hallway. She takes off her shoes and places them in their spot on the shoe rack before hanging up her work bag.

"I get it I do, but that doesn't mean I have to like it". No response. She glances down at her phone and see Dean hung up on her. She takes a sharp intake and steadies herself. One, two, three and then releases her breath. Calmness washes over her like a blanket of security and she shuffles into the living room before stopping abruptly. Dean. Stood in their living room. His dark hair tousled and dark circles under his eyes, but they light up when she sees him. Her heart hammers in her chest as she races towards him before jumping in his arms and wrapping her legs around his waist. He murmurs in approval and his hands rest on her ass as she nuzzles into his chest.

"Hey darling", he whispers before placing her back on her feet. He holds her at arm length and his eyes flicker over her face. She looks up at him with big eyes, as if she can't believe he is really here.

"I thought you had a meeting", she asks quizzically.

"I did, I still do, but I don't want to be anywhere that you're not."

"You quit your job? Dean! We talked about this; we'd find a way to make it work that didn't involve the other one sacrificing their job." She scolds him lightly but doesn't say anything further, waiting for his response. He lets go of her arms and slowly lowers one knee to the floor.

"Dean? What... what are you doing?"

"I have loved you from the day we first met, even if you did spill coffee over me" he says with a gentle laugh. "I have never wanted anything so badly in my life, you have changed me for the better and you know exactly what to do and say to challenge me in the best way. I never want to be apart from you again, and us doing long distance has solidified that. We will figure this out but Phoebe, will you do the biggest honour of my life and be my wife?", Dean says with tears in his eyes as he looks up at her. Phoebe's heart stops and she stares down at the man on his knees for her, staring at her with so much adoration in his eyes. This man has never questioned herself worth, never made her to feel anything less than she is, helped put her back together after she had been shattered.

"Say something, please Darling?", a slight hitch in his breath is all she needs to know he is just as nervous as she is. She slowly gets to her knees, and grabs his face in a gentle grip, running her fingertips over his cheeks. She bumps her nose against his and whispers, "I'd be honoured to marry you Dean". His mouth crashes against hers with bruising force and he tangles his hand in her hair, pulling slightly before detaching their lips from one another.

"You've just made me the happiest man in the universe Squidge, and I promise you; I will try and make you the happiest I can every day of our beautiful lives together", he says with such earnest that Phoebe doesn't doubt him for a second. She grabs his hand and pulls him to his feet before leading him to the bedroom, gasping as she walks in. Rose and lily petals cover the sheets and a banner above the bed says, 'happily engaged'. She turns to look at him, giggling as she says "well, it's a good thing I said yes isn't it?". Dean nods happily before pulling his suit jacket off and then his white button up shirt. He walks her backwards to the bed before her knees bang softly against the edge, forcing her to sit. She looks up at him before moving back on the bed, curling her finger, beckoning him to get on the bed with her.

"How could I ever deny my fiancé what she wants", he pronounces with a sheepish grin on his face, as he crawls above her and then dips his head, capturing her lips in a passionate kiss. Their teeth bash together and Phoebe lets out a soft moan when Dean traces a path from behind her ear to her collar bone with his fingers. Her back arches and he pulls off her shirt before grabbing her breast in his hand as he continues to kiss her. Soft groans escape his mouth as his other hand starts creeping down towards the waistband of her jeans. Dean breaks the kiss to look at Phoebe, his dark eyes searching hers for clarification. Phoebe blushes and nods before moving his hand down her jeans.

"I want these off", she gasps out.

"Anything you want darling", Dean says with a husky voice and slowly pulls down her jeans. Phoebe huffs as he takes his time and starts to wiggle the jeans down herself but stops when Dean pins her with a hard look. He continues his slow decent of her jeans, running his eyes over her scars with adoration and love. Heat creeps up her face at his hard stare and pulls at his arms, trying to get him to go faster.

"Nothing is going to stop me from taking my time and appreciating the beauty in front of me Phoebe. I have waited so long to be back in your arms", he says with sincerity in his voice. The jeans fall off the end of the bed and Dean's fingers slowly rub over her clit, causing Phoebe to groan out in pleasure. Tingles flow throughout her body and her toes curl.

"So responsive for me darling", moving her panties to the side and pushing the tip of his index finger between her folds, feeling how wet she is. Phoebe whimpers and her hips buck, trying to gain more friction but Deans rough hands pin her hips down. A brief look of concern flashes over Phoebes face before she relaxes and pulls Dean by the back of his head so their lips meet again. Dean groans into her mouth as he eases his finger into her walls, feeling them clamp and trying to pull his fingers further in. His lips leave hers to run his teeth over her nipple, biting and sucking gently, feeling her hips buck and her writhing below him. She gasps in pleasure and pulls at his jeans, and with one hand, Dean quickly removes them and Phoebe quickly grabs his length in her hands, pumping slowly. One finger slips over the tip, and Dean thrusts slowly in her hand before pulling it out of her grasp and moving down her body. His lips flick over her clit and Phoebe lets out a shrill moan, and Dean smiles against her folds before pushing his tongue in. The rough surface of his tongue touches the velvety feeling of her walls and Phoebe moans incoherently, grabbing the back of his head and holding him there as she grinds herself onto his face. Pride floods Dean as she takes what she wants from him, but when he feels her walls flutter, he pulls back with a wicked grin on his face.

"Dean, no please, I'm so close", she huffs out in frustration.

"The only way you're coming tonight is if it's all over my cock, darling", Dean says as he pushes the tip of his cock along her folds and Phoebe arches her back, rubbing her nipples over his chest. He slowly pushes into her and groans at the feeling of her clamping down on him. His head falls into her neck and nips at the skin there as Phoebe's legs wrap around his waist and she rocks into him, but not quick enough. His hips snap forward, causing Phoebe to gasp out as the last of Dean's patience shreds. He sets a relentless pace and moans bounce off the walls as the sound of skin snapping together floods the bedroom.

"Come with me darling, I'm so close", Dean says as he keeps up the pace but his finger drifts down and strokes lightly over Phoebe's clit, knowing she's close to being overstimulated. She whimpers in his arms and clamps down on his cock, before moaning as she gushes around him. He lets out a grunt as he feels himself spill inside her, staying there for a few seconds before collapsing in the bed next to her. Dean pulls Phoebe into a warm embrace, brushing her sweat soaked her out of her face before kissing her on the forehead. She nuzzles into him before speaking, "in this life and every after?".

"Always darling."

Chapter Twenty

A year later

Phoebe steps out of the dressing room, with the help of the seamstress that Dean hired.

"Phoebe! You look absolutely amazing. Dean is going to fall over when he sees you walk down that aisle." Soft makeup highlights her features, making her eyes light up and a hand rests on her shoulder. Phoebe turns to look in the mirror, her eyes going wide as she takes in her appearance. Her long red hair tied into a braid running down her back. She touches the hand on her shoulder, giving it a little squeeze before running her hands down the white dress, her fingers brushing over the beautiful flowers that had been woven into the body of the dress. The lace of the dress sits delicately across her chest and her eyes drop to the small amount of cleavage on show, blush creeping over her chest and up the back of her neck.

"Oh stop it, you look good enough to eat, If you swung both ways then Dean wouldn't have had a chance", Jessica lets out a laugh at the look of disbelief on Phoebe's face.

"Only you would think to say that on mine and Dean's wedding day", Phoebe says with a soft giggle. She turns to look at Jessica and pulls her into a warm embrace. She feels her fingers brush up against her scars accidently, but Phoebe doesn't say anything, having learnt to slowly love the scars the cover her body, thanks to Dean.

"Are you ready to be married? Coz if not, I've got a getaway car", Jessica says with a snort but with a hint of sincerity that Phoebe knows that if she said yes then Jessica would do it in a heartbeat. She nods happily and looks towards the doors leading to the chapel, tension tightening in her stomach before she lets out a deep breath and grabs her flowers from the vase. The oranges and yellows of the sunflowers compliment her hair and Jessica threads one through Phoebe's hair as they start to hear the sound of everyone slowly rising to their feet as the bridal march begins being played on the violins. Tears fill both Phoebe's and Jessica's eyes as they look at each other.

"I never thought you'd get married to someone", Jessica admits as she brushes a stray hair out of Phoebe's face.

"Neither did i", Phoebe responds, "I just wish I'd let Dean in sooner so that we both could have been happier for longer."

"Don't talk about yourself like that. You did what you thought was best at the time. Now hurry up and let's get you married before Dean thinks you have run off."

They link arms just as the doors are opened and they slowly start to walk down the aisle. Phoebe risks a look up at Dean, and her heart lurches in her chest. His dark green suit makes his eyes pop and as she stares at him, she sees tears escape down his cheeks and she smiles reassuringly as tears creep into her own eyes. As they reach the altar, Jessica kisses Phoebe on the cheek before taking the bouquet off of her and placing Phoebe's hand in Deans. He grabs it and nods at Jessica as she takes her seat at the front of the congregation, standing next to Piper, sniffling and dabbing at her eyes with a tissue. Phoebe allows Dean to pull her in front of everyone and she focuses on his eyes as the priest starts speaking.

"Dearly beloved, we are gathered here today to witness the marriage between Phoebe and Dean. If anyone has any objections please speak now, or forever hold your peace." Dean and Jessica both turn and pin the guests with a hard glare and everyone lets out a nervous giggle. The priest waits a moment before talking about God and how he is blessed that Phoebe and Dean have come together despite all the obstacles.

"And now for the vows", the priest says before turning to Dean. He grabs Phoebes hands, and as Jack brings forward the vows, Dean gently shakes his head.

"Phoebe, I never thought we would be here. I thought that we would never work and that I would die alone. But you showed me that it's okay to show weakness and to let people in. The moment I first saw you, I knew you were the one, but I couldn't move too fast with you. I knew there was more than to you than meets the eye, and you have proven how strong you are time and time again. I am going to spend the rest of my life with you and trying to be the man you deserve. I can't wait to grow old together and have children and grandchildren. I hope to make you as happy as you have made me." Tears stream down both Phoebe's and Dean's face, and Phoebe lets out a shaky breath as she recites hers from memory.

"Dean, from the moment I first saw you, I wanted you in my life so bad that I didn't know what to do. You have shown me what love and life is supposed to look like. It's not meant to be anxiety and PTSD attacks, its meant to be with the person who makes you whole and you were like the missing piece of the puzzle. I never want to be with anyone else; you are it for me. When I first met you, it was like I was drowning but then when we went on that first date, it was you saving me without realising. You never judged me for my past or the trauma I've been through. You helped me through it at my own pace and you never pushed me, and for that I will forever be grateful. I will try to spend the rest of my life making you as happy as you make me." Their hands tighten around each other, and the ring bearers bring up the rings and they each slowly slip the rings onto each other. Phoebe and Dean never take their eyes off of each other and the priest declares them married.

"You may now kiss the bride", the priest announces.

"About time", Dean murmurs loud enough for the congregation to hear and they let out a laugh as Dean dips Phoebe and kisses her passionately.

"In this life and every after?" she speaks against him.

"Always darling".

Epilogue

A giggle escapes from Phoebe's lips as she watches Dean chase Sam round the playground before grabbing and tickling him; his feet kicking in the air as he screams in happiness. Phoebe's hands run over her stomach, protective over the second child growing in her stomach, Dean and Phoebe already wrapped around the little girls finger. The two males run around each other, well Dean walking on his knees to give little Sammy a fighting chance, and they both look over at Phoebe, their eyes twinkling with the same mischievous glint.

"Uh oh", she mutters before very slowly backing up, despite the massive grin on her face. The boys run towards her and she pretends to be scared as she gently drops to her knees and begs for mercy, but the boys barrel into her, being careful of her belly mind you, and tackle her with kisses and hugs and tickles. She laughs hysterically and Dean kisses her neck before leaning down and kissing her belly, watching in astonishment as Sam kisses the bump too.

"I'll always protect you", the boy mutters and the parents heart warm with him already being protective of her. They had worries that he would be jealous of her but he had bounced up and down when they told him he was going to have a baby sister. With that, they all stand hand in hand and walk up the garden to the house, ready for family night and dinner. Phoebe lets out a sigh of contentment and Dean eyes her warily whilst also keeping an eye on Sam.

"What's wrong darling?"

"Nothing, I am happy and even more so knowing I have you and my two precious babies in my life."

"Am I not a precious baby?", he feigns disbelief, knowing it will get a small giggle out of Phoebe, one of his favourite noises that she makes.

"Of course you are, but you're the love of my life, so you're in a whole other category." He smiles and walks her through the door, before helping Phoebe onto the sofa, and Sam walks in with a cup of water which he hands to Phoebe. She sighs in happiness and watches the boys walk off to the kitchen and start preparing dinner. Life couldn't get any better than this.

Blurb

When Phoebe meets Joel, she believes he is the love of her life. But when the first punch is thrown, she knows she has to get out of the relationship.

Fast forward 2 years, she meets Dean and she is drawn to him like a moth to a flame. But they both have baggage. Can they both overcome their trauma? Can they jump through every hurdle to be together? And when the past comes knocking, will they be able to defeat it?